EVERY SECRET LEADS TO ANOTHER

SECRETS *of the* MANOR

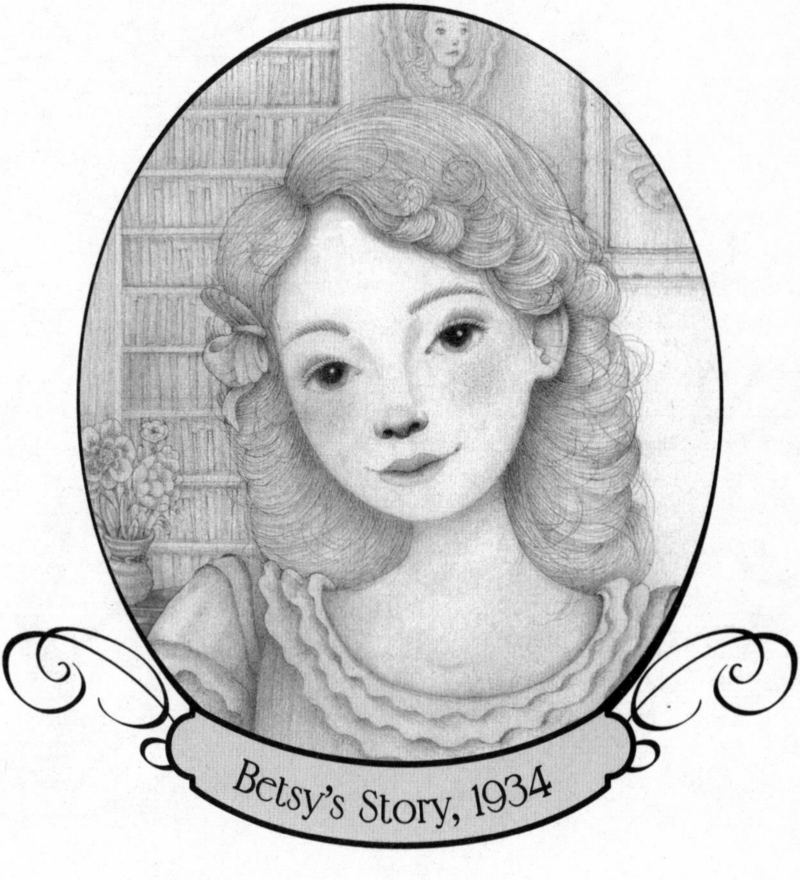

BY

ADELE WHITBY

Simon Spotlight
New York London Toronto Sydney New Delhi

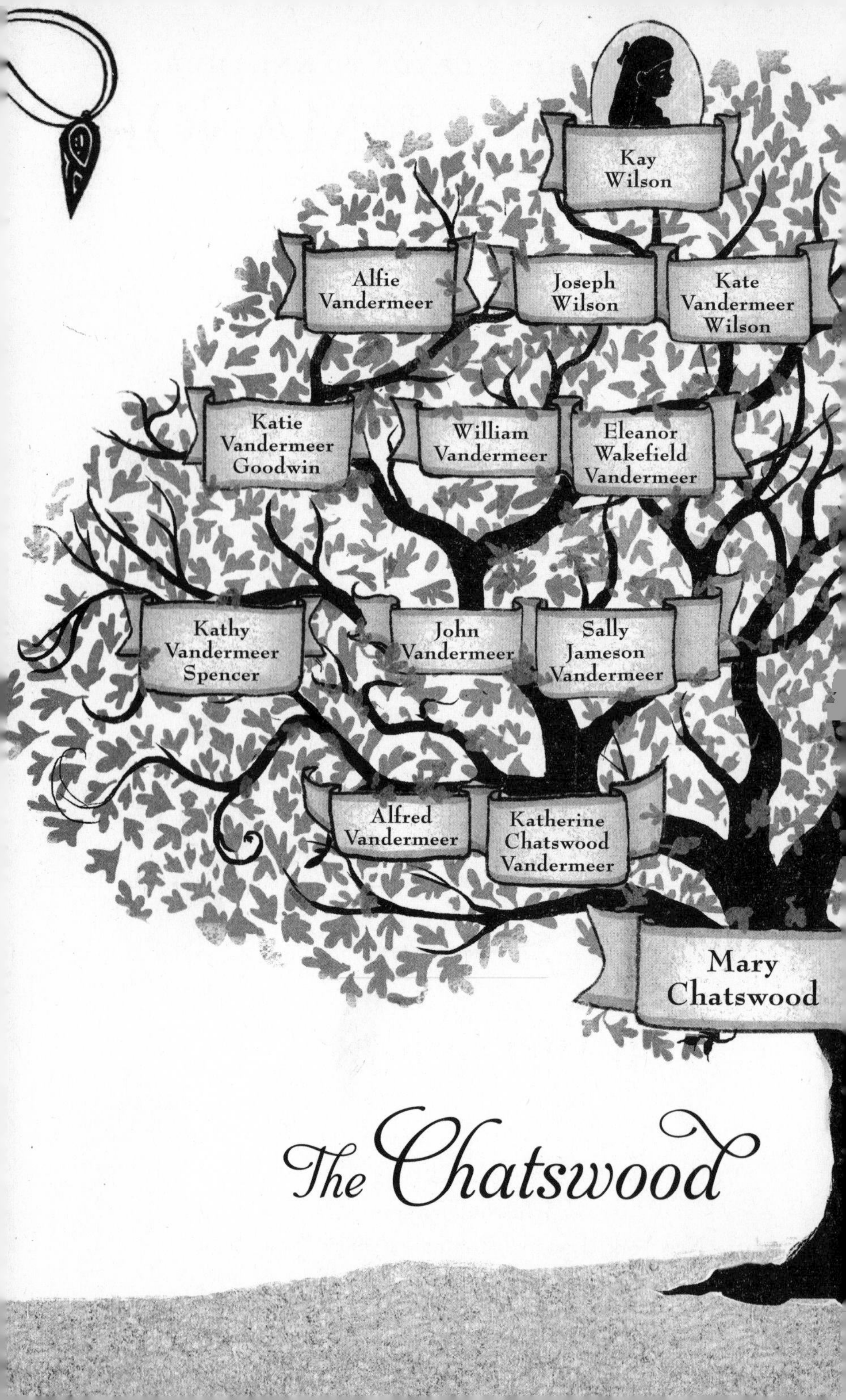
Kay Wilson
Alfie Vandermeer
Joseph Wilson
Kate Vandermeer Wilson
Katie Vandermeer Goodwin
William Vandermeer
Eleanor Wakefield Vandermeer
Kathy Vandermeer Spencer
John Vandermeer
Sally Jameson Vandermeer
Alfred Vandermeer
Katherine Chatswood Vandermeer
Mary Chatswood
The Chatswood

Family Tree

Beth Northrop
Beth Etheridge Northrop
James Northrop
Gabrielle Trufant
Liz Burns Etheridge
Edwin Etheridge
Beatrice Etheridge Trufant
Claude Trufant
Eliza Tynne Burns
Douglas Burns
Edward Etheridge
Charlotte Gordon Etheridge
Elizabeth Chatswood Tynne
Maxwell Tynne
Cecily Smith Etheridge
George Etheridge
Robert Chatswood

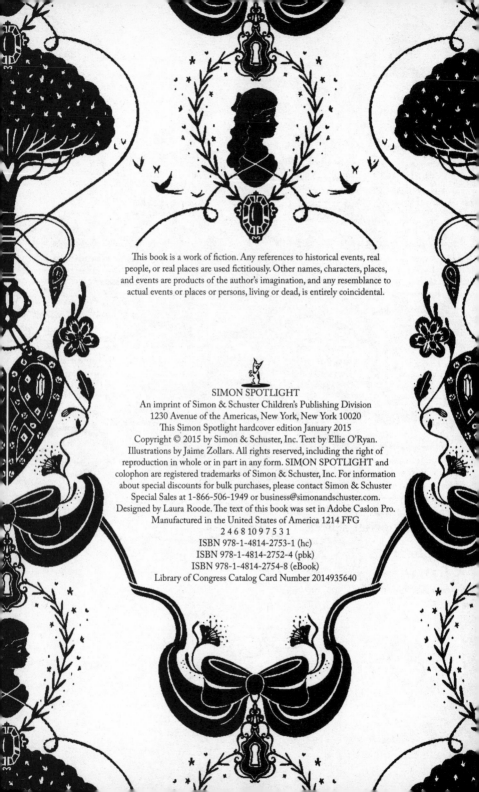

This book is a work of fiction. Any references to historical events, real people, or real places are used fictitiously. Other names, characters, places, and events are products of the author's imagination, and any resemblance to actual events or places or persons, living or dead, is entirely coincidental.

SIMON SPOTLIGHT
An imprint of Simon & Schuster Children's Publishing Division
1230 Avenue of the Americas, New York, New York 10020
This Simon Spotlight hardcover edition January 2015

Designed by Laura Roode. The text of this book was set in Adobe Caslon Pro.
Manufactured in the United States of America 1214 FFG
2 4 6 8 10 9 7 5 3 1
ISBN 978-1-4814-2753-1 (hc)
ISBN 978-1-4814-2752-4 (pbk)
ISBN 978-1-4814-2754-8 (eBook)
Library of Congress Catalog Card Number 2014935640

1

Voilà!" Madame Lorraine exclaimed as she stepped away from the dais. "You may open your eyes, Lady Betsy."

My breath caught in my chest. For weeks, Madame Lorraine, the famous Parisian dressmaker, had been working on a custom gown for my twelfth birthday ball—which was less than a month away! And now the gown was nearly ready; all that was left for Madame Lorraine to do was add the trim. I kept my eyes shut for another second to savor the anticipation.

Then I looked in the mirror.

Was that really me looking back?

My new ball gown was the most gorgeous dress I'd ever seen. It was the color of the sky on a summery day; Madame Lorraine had ordered the shimmery silk charmeuse fabric all the way from China. The gown had capped sleeves and a fluttery skirt that hit just below my knees. Madame Lorraine's creation was more gorgeous than I'd imagined it could be. And it wasn't even finished yet!

I shivered—just the tiniest bit, really—but Mum noticed, of course, like she always noticed everything.

"Have you taken a chill, Betsy?" she asked, nodding at the goose prickles on my bare arms.

"A little," I replied. "But mostly I'm excited!"

A knowing smile crossed Mum's face. "Of course you are," she said. Then she nodded at my new lady's maid, Maggie. "But perhaps it is a bit too drafty in here for a fitting."

Mum didn't need to say another word; Maggie immediately crossed the room to close the windows. The April sunshine was so bright and cheery that we'd all wanted to enjoy it through the open windows without giving much thought to the chill in the morning air.

"It's coming along beautifully, Madame Lorraine," Mum continued. "What a lovely silhouette! So very modern."

"*Merci*, Lady Beth," said Madame Lorraine. "Have

you and Lady Betsy selected the embellishments?"

"Yes, we have," Mum replied. "We adore the velvet ribbon, but the satin ribbon will be more appropriate for the season. And while the purple beads have a lovely sheen, they don't hold a candle to the gold ones. Nellie, would you please fetch them?"

"Certainly, milady," Nellie, Mum's lady's maid, replied. Madame Lorraine had brought an entire trunk of trim with her—rolls of ribbons in every color, sparkling beads and rhinestones, and silk flowers more delicate than anything in the garden. It had been almost impossible to choose! In the end, though, Mum and I had both agreed that the shiny satin ribbon and sparkly gold beads would be just the thing to complement the gown—and the Elizabeth necklace, a precious family heirloom that I would receive on the day I turned twelve.

Every firstborn daughter in my family had been named Elizabeth in honor of my great-great-grandmother Elizabeth, who had been born almost one hundred years ago. We took different variations on the name "Elizabeth" for our nicknames—I went by Betsy, for example, while my mum went by Beth—but we were all Elizabeths, just like her. But there was even more to the family legacy than our names. There was the Elizabeth necklace.

When Great-Great-Grandmother Elizabeth turned twelve, she received a stunning gold pendant in the shape of half a heart, which was set with brilliant blue sapphires. Elizabeth's twin sister, Katherine, had received a nearly identical necklace, but it was set with fiery red rubies instead. The necklaces weren't just beautiful; they were deeply significant to each twin, since they were carefully chosen by their beloved mother, who died just a few months before their birthday. Their mother didn't live to celebrate their birthdays with them, so the special gift she left for each of them became their most cherished possession.

When the two pendants were put together, they formed a single, whole heart, which was a perfect symbol for Elizabeth and Katherine, as they were almost never apart. But after the girls grew up, family obligations forced them to separate. As the slightly older twin, Elizabeth had been pledged to marry her cousin, Maxwell Tynne, in order to keep Chatswood Manor in the family. Meanwhile, Katherine had fallen in love with Alfred Vandermeer, and shortly after marrying, they emigrated from England to America, where her new husband founded Vandermeer Steel. The family lived in the beautiful and stately Vandermeer Manor, overlooking the ocean in Rhode Island. That's where my cousin Kay Vandermeer Wilson, Katherine's great-great-granddaughter, lived today. Kay and I weren't just cousins; we were best friends, even though we'd never met. We had so much in common—we both loved *Hollywood Hello* magazine (me for the articles about radio plays, Kay for the photos of movie stars), dogs were our favorite animals, and our birthdays were just a month apart. And in two weeks, Kay and I would finally meet when she and her parents—Aunt Kate and Uncle Joseph—arrived in England to help celebrate my birthday! I already knew that meeting Cousin Kay for the first time would be the very best birthday present of all.

And to make things even more exciting, Mum and Aunt Kate had promised to tell Kay and me a secret on my birthday. A *big* secret that had been in the Chatswood family for generations. For months now, Kay and I had been trying to find out what it was. But neither Mum nor Aunt Kate would say another word about it. The suspense was driving us mad!

I shifted my weight ever so slightly as Mum and Madame Lorraine discussed the trim we'd selected.

"I think some beads around the neck, *oui,* and perhaps the sleeves," Madame Lorraine said through a mouthful of pins. "Not too much, of course. Nothing ostentatious. A beauty like Lady Betsy needs no adornment; she will shine all on her own!"

I flushed with pleasure at the compliment. It was an honor to have Madame Lorraine design my ball gown. My mother's French cousin, Gabrielle, had surprised us by insisting that Madame Lorraine, her personal dressmaker, travel all the way to Chatswood Manor just to make my special birthday dress. In a few weeks, Cousin Gabrielle would also be joining us for the birthday festivities. I scarcely knew Gabrielle, whose glamorous life in Paris kept her too busy for country holidays at Chatswood Manor, but I was excited about having a house full of visitors. Ever since my father died when I was just a baby, Mum and I had been on our own. We made a good team—Mum and I did almost everything together—but sometimes I secretly wished that our little family were larger. What a change it would be to have the Wilsons and Cousin Gabrielle at Chatswood Manor! Just the thought of laughter at breakfast and cozy evenings in the parlor made me smile. I knew Mum was as eager as I was for our extended family to arrive.

"You know, I am having another thought," Madame Lorraine mused. She snipped a length of ribbon off the roll, her silver scissors flashing in the sunlight. "What if we add a belt from this ribbon, like so? I will make a buckle to match . . . perhaps even embroider some beads on it. . . ."

"A belt? Instead of a sash?" Mum said, frowning a little. "Wouldn't that be a bit casual?"

"*Non, non.* I can assure you, it is the very latest fashion in Paris," replied Madame Lorraine.

"What do you think, Betsy?" Mum asked me.

"Yes! I love that idea," I said. "I think a beaded belt would be smashing."

"How much times have changed since my own birthday ball," Mum said. "My gown was blue as well, but entirely different in style. It was full length, with a gorgeous overskirt made of shimmery tulle. And I wore gloves with my gown, of course—gloves that stretched all the way past my elbows."

"Ahh, *oui,* gloves for Lady Betsy as well, I think," Madame Lorraine said.

"Well, I'm glad to know that fashions haven't changed *that* much," Mum said with a laugh.

"I remember when Miss Kate—I suppose I should call her Mrs. Wilson—was getting ready for her twelfth birthday ball," Nellie reminisced. "She *hated* her fittings—called them frightfully dull wastes of time. The dressmaker was forever begging her to stand still!"

We all laughed—even Madame Lorraine.

"Then one day, I started reading to Miss Kate to take her mind off the torture of her fittings," Nellie continued. "It did the trick. We had a bit of a reading club back then. Oh, we loved stories more than anyone else in Vandermeer Manor."

"But not more than me," I teased. "Tell me the story, Nellie, of how you came to England. Please!" I always wanted to hear about how Mum's maid, Shannon, had fallen in love with the Vandermeers' chauffeur, Hank, when Mum had visited Aunt Kate as a girl. Rather than watch Shannon return to England and leave true love behind, Mum and Aunt Kate had conspired to help Nellie and Shannon switch places! It was a thrilling and romantic tale, the sort of story I would expect to hear on the radio during one of my favorite programs. I could hardly believe it had happened in real life!

"A favorite story, to be sure," Mum said, "but I think some refreshments are in order first. Would you mind fetching a tray from the kitchen?"

"I'll go," Maggie volunteered.

"No, no. You stay in case Lady Betsy needs anything," Nellie said. "I'll be back in a jiffy."

"There," Madame Lorraine announced. "What do you think of the belt? I will add the beads later, of course."

"Oh, it's perfect!" I cried.

"Very cunning," Mum said, sounding pleased. "The perfect accoutrement!"

There was a soft rap at the door. It was one of the footmen, Adam.

"Beg your pardon, milady," he said to Mum, "but you've a telephone call. Long-distance, from America."

"America!" I cried. "It's got to be Aunt Kate!"

2

In one swift motion, Mum rose to her feet. "If you'll excuse me, Madame Lorraine," she said smoothly. "But I must take this call."

"Mum! Wait for me!" I spoke up.

But she had already hurried out of the room.

I jumped off the dais and felt a dozen pins stab me where Madame Lorraine had placed the ribbon. "Ow!" I cried.

"Wait, please, *mademoiselle*," Madame Lorraine urged. "Do not move until I loosen the pins."

"Maggie, would you help her, please?" I said. It was a rare treat to talk to our American relatives on the phone, and I didn't want to miss a moment of it. Mum always let me sit beside her and listen to her part of the conversation. And best of all, sometimes Mum even let me say hello to Cousin Kay!

The seconds ticked away while Maggie and Madame Lorraine loosened the pins enough for me to wriggle out of the gown.

"Would you like to wear your pink dress again, Lady Betsy?" Maggie asked, moving slower than a swan as she reached for the dress I'd chosen that morning. "Or did you have another ensemble in mind for the afternoon?"

I took one look at the dainty buttons on the dress and shook my head. "There's no time for that," I replied as I reached for my silk dressing gown. I flung the gown over my starched white slip and bolted from the room, tying the sash as I hurried down the stairs toward the library. There I found Mum, holding on to the edge of her oak desk as if to steady herself.

"Oh, Kate," she said into the receiver. "Oh, no . . ."

The expression on Mum's face—a strangled look of shock and dismay—was not one I would soon forget. I just knew that the news was bad. *Oh, please,* I thought. *Not Kay. Not Uncle Joseph. Please let them be all right.*

Without saying a word, I reached for Mum's hand. She was so engrossed in the call that I don't think she noticed me until she felt the warmth of my touch.

Mum pulled her hand from my grasp and covered the mouthpiece.

"Betsy, I need to speak privately with Aunt Kate."

"But I—"

"Not now," she said firmly.

Then Mum returned to the telephone, keeping her eyes fixed on me as I left the library. She didn't start speaking again until I reached the door.

I stood alone in the hallway, stunned, trying to understand what had just happened. Mum had never asked me to leave the library while she was on the telephone—*never*. And especially not when she was talking to Aunt Kate! Something terrible must have happened, and the longer I stood there, the heavier my worries grew. How could I possibly wait until Mum was off the phone to find out what had happened?

Suddenly, I realized that my hand was still on the doorknob. And the door was still open a crack. In my shock, I had neglected to close it all the way.

If I leaned forward—if I didn't make a single sound—it was entirely possible that I could still hear Mum's part of the conversation.

It wouldn't be wrong to listen in, I tried to convince

myself. *Mum and I don't have secrets from each other. Not even one. And I'm sure she'll tell me everything later, anyway. She always does.*

Holding my breath, I leaned toward the sliver of light peeking through the crack. Sure enough, I could hear Mum's voice if I strained my ears. I concentrated all my energy on listening, doing my best to ignore the guilt pricking at my conscience.

"But, Kate, I don't know why he would—surely he *knew*—of course, of course—"

"Lady Betsy!"

I spun around as if I'd been caught with my hand in the cookie jar. Maggie had crept up behind me so quietly that I hadn't even noticed her—not until her words pierced my ears. *Oh, no—what if Mum heard her too?* I wondered.

"You're not—you're not *listening* at the door, are you?" Maggie continued, altogether too loud for my liking.

Annoyance burned inside me. "Shhh!" I hissed as I pulled Maggie down the hall. "I wasn't—Mum never keeps her phone calls with Aunt Kate a secret from me. I was just—"

Maggie's nose crinkled into a disapproving frown. *Oh, come now,* I thought to myself. *There's no need for her to look so scandalized.*

"Then why weren't you in the room with her, milady?"

My mouth opened and closed, for I didn't have a satisfactory answer at the ready. Maggie must've sensed that, because she put her arm around my back and began to guide me to my room.

"Listening at doors is beneath a young lady of your stature," Maggie said in a gentle voice, but my cheeks still burned with embarrassment. "Come along, Lady Betsy. Madame Lorraine is still in your room, and it's not right to lurk in corridors and keep her waiting."

I spoke not one word to Maggie for the entire walk back to my room, thinking that there would be no better way to express my displeasure with her. Not for the first time, I found myself wishing that my former lady's maid, Emily, was by my side instead. It was five weeks since Emily had retired from service, and not a day went by that I didn't miss her. Emily knew me better than anyone else (except for Mum, of course). *She* would've understood that I wasn't *really* eavesdropping.

She would've understood how unbearable it was to wait for information about the troubling news from America.

I kept my silence even after Madame Lorraine had returned to her work, snipping and pinning lengths of the silky ribbon to my gown. Meanwhile, Maggie studiously examined all the dresses in my wardrobe, setting aside the winter ones that I would no longer wear now that spring had arrived. Several long minutes passed like this until Mum finally returned to the room. One look at her face told me that she'd been crying, though she was as composed as usual.

"Well!" she said, with forced cheer in her voice. "Where are we, Madame Lorraine?"

"Mum, what did Aunt Kate say?" I said. "Is everything all right? Please tell me. I've been so worried."

Mum looked at me with red-rimmed eyes. "Yes, Betsy, of course. I would prefer to tell you this later, after your fitting is done, but I do hate to see you so distressed and you've a right to know. . . ."

Her voice trailed off as a thoughtful expression crossed her face, leaving me in agony until she spoke again.

"There's no easy way to tell you this, my dear," Mum finally said. "Our cousins' circumstances are dire, and they will not be able to attend your birthday ball."

"Mum, no!" I cried. "How can—I don't understand." The plans for Cousin Kay and her parents to travel to England for my birthday had been made months ago. What could have happened to alter them now, when my birthday was just a few weeks away?

"I'm afraid that's not all," Mum continued. "In addition, they've had to cancel Cousin Kay's birthday ball."

Poor Kay! My eyes filled with tears. "How did this happen?" I asked, my voice strained from the lump in my throat.

"It's partly the Depression, darling," Mum said. "Do you remember what I told you about it?"

I nodded slowly. It was very complicated stuff, tricky to understand, but a few years back the stock market in New York had crashed, and fortunes were lost around the globe. Then jobs were lost, and homes, until people on every continent were struggling. The *Times* had just begun to report about the first hopeful signs of recovery here in England, but in America, things were far worse; an enormous number of Americans were still living in poverty. Many of them had nothing to eat and nowhere to live. There had even been a photograph in the newspaper of a breadline, where small children waited for hours in hopes of getting something to eat. It was their little feet that I couldn't forget: shoeless, smudged with dirt from the gutter.

"But . . ." My voice trailed off as I searched for the right words. "But the Vandermeers are the wealthiest family in Rhode Island. Vandermeer Steel is one of the largest steel manufacturers in the country!"

Mum sighed. "Vandermeer Steel is burdened with debt that it cannot possibly repay right now," she explained. "When Aunt Kate's father died, her brother—Uncle Alfie—became the president of Vandermeer Steel. Unfortunately, Uncle Alfie embarked on several foolish ventures that have imperiled Vandermeer Steel and devastated the family fortune."

"Like what?" I asked, horrified.

"I'm afraid I'm not entirely clear on the details," Mum said. "Aunt Kate was so upset that it wasn't the right time for me to ask questions."

"But couldn't Uncle Joseph get a loan from the bank?" I asked.

"Unfortunately, that's no longer an option," Mum said. "Many banks were the first to succumb to the ravages of the Depression. And the banks that have managed to survive are now hoarding their cash and refusing to loan it. It is quite impossible for almost anyone in America, even someone as successful as your uncle, to obtain a loan right now."

"I—I—I don't understand how this *happened*!" I cried. "It's all so—so—so sudden."

"It only seems that way, Betsy," Mum explained sadly. "But this terrible outcome was years in the making, ever since Uncle Alfie took over Vandermeer Steel. I know that Uncle Joseph is doing his best to make things right. He has tried . . . everything . . . he could think of to save Vandermeer Steel from its creditors, even mortgaging Vandermeer Manor."

I stood a little straighter. "Mortgaging Vandermeer Manor? But that's their home! Where will they go?"

"They've already moved into one of the guest cottages," Mum said quietly. "They had no choice. Apparently, the entire staff was let go last week. Aunt

Kate is preparing for the possibility that they will lose Vandermeer Manor in its entirety."

"But where will they live?"

"They still have the town house in New York," Mum told me. "And if they can sell that, they should have the funds they need to rent a small apartment."

Poor Kay, I thought again. She must've felt like her entire world was slipping away from her. "Mum, would you ring them back?" I asked urgently. "Please, I want to speak with Kay."

"I would if I could, Betsy," Mum said. "But they've disconnected their telephone to save on expenses. That's one of the reasons why Aunt Kate called. In fact, our call was dropped before Kate and I could even say good-bye."

And then my strong mother's voice faltered, and her eyes filled with tears.

"Mum!"

She sniffed quickly and dabbed at her eyes with a handkerchief. "Forgive me, Betsy. It was a—it was a very difficult phone call. But we mustn't forget that Aunt Kate is as brave as her great-grandmother Katherine, who had the strength to forge a new life in

America. And I've no doubt that Kay is just as strong. No matter what comes to pass, they will find a way to endure—and overcome."

"I wish I could talk to Kay," I said. "I wish I could tell her how sorry I am that this has happened."

"You could write to her," Mum suggested. "Aunt Kate promised she'd send a telegram with their new address as soon as the fate of Vandermeer Manor is settled."

I nodded. "I'll write a letter right now and post it as soon as the telegram arrives." Suddenly, an idea occurred to me. "Mum! Couldn't we send them some money?"

Mum sighed. "I've offered, Betsy. Of course I've offered," she replied. "But Aunt Kate always refused. She didn't know how dire it was. The accounts of a large estate can be very complicated to follow, and as we know now, Uncle Joseph was . . ."

"What?" I asked. "Uncle Joseph was what?"

Mum shook her head, and I had the feeling she'd changed her mind about telling me something. "I—I believe that he was trying to shield Aunt Kate from the harsh realities in hopes that he could protect her."

"Well, that was very foolish of him," I said hotly.

"It's not our place to judge," Mum said gently. "Misfortune can strike when one least expects it, Betsy. It's not for us to say what could have been done or should have been done."

There was a heaviness in her voice that caught my attention, and when I looked at Mum, I saw that her forehead was creased into deep furrows. A terrible feeling of dread began to gnaw at me.

"Mum?" I asked slowly. "Are . . . we . . . ? Are our finances . . . sound?"

For a moment, Mum stared past me, as if she hadn't heard the question. Then she shook herself slightly and reached for my hand. "Betsy, you mustn't worry about such things," she told me. "Our fortune is fully intact, and Chatswood Manor is in no trouble at all."

"Are you certain?"

"Really, my dear, you must take me at my word," she said, and her voice sounded more sure this time. "I'll be honest that many great estates have been struggling under the current financial climate, but Chatswood is not one of them."

I stared at Mum, but she didn't meet my eye.

Instead, she reached down and picked an imaginary speck of dust off my dress. Something was wrong . . . but what?

"Mum?" I asked. "Is there something you're not telling me?"

I held my breath, waiting, until she finally spoke. "Yes, Betsy, there is," Mum said at last. "But you've got to trust me that it's for the best that I don't tell you right now."

"Please tell me now!"

"Betsy, have faith. It's a complicated situation, but I'm going to handle it. To discuss it with you now would only make you worry for no reason, and I won't have that."

"If you can't tell me what it is, can you at least tell me the secret?"

"The secret? What secret?" Mum said, confused.

"The one you and Aunt Kate were going to tell Kay and me," I reminded her. "The important family secret we had to wait to find out."

A look of understanding crossed Mum's face. "Oh. You know, Betsy, Kate and I didn't even have a chance to discuss it," she said. "And I can't imagine telling you without her and Kay present. I'm afraid you'll just have to wait until Kate and I speak again."

Mum reached forward to stroke my cheek. "I must excuse myself now; I'm sure you remember that the advisers are coming for their seasonal inspection today, and I'd like to review the accounts before they arrive. Betsy, do enjoy the rest of your fitting. I'm sorry to mar it with such unpleasant news, but I have the utmost faith that Kay and her parents will overcome this trying period. And we'll offer whatever help they'll accept."

"Yes, Mum," I said.

But as soon as she was gone, I stared at my reflection in the mirror. My beautiful ball gown seemed altogether changed. Whenever I moved, the shimmery fabric twinkled as if it were showing off, a horribly gaudy display that made me feel ashamed. And look at what had captured my attention all morning: satin ribbon or velvet, purple beads or gold. *What right do I have to wear a dress like this?* I wondered. *What right do I have to dance at my birthday ball when Cousin Kay doesn't even know where she'll be living in a month?*

It was utterly insensitive. No, it was worse. It was selfish.

"Madame Lorraine," I said. "I'm afraid that I've got a headache. I'm terribly sorry to trouble you, but might we continue tomorrow?"

"*Oui,* of course, Lady Betsy," she said at once. "I hope some rest will restore you. A fitting is a very trying endeavor."

Not as trying as having your family fall into despair, I thought, with Cousin Kay still very much on my mind. *Not as trying as losing your family home.*

It took several minutes for Madame Lorraine and Maggie to free me from the gown and all the pins that held the ribbon embellishments in place. I stared at my reflection the entire time, torn between my love for the dress and my sudden shame of having something so beautiful—and so expensive—when there were people in the world struggling to survive.

Including, perhaps, my dear cousin.

It's not fair, a small voice inside me said. *It's not fair, and you know it. Why should you have a fine gown—and not Kay? Why should you have a birthday ball—and not Kay? The ball has been a family tradition for generations. It's not right for the Elizabeth heir to enjoy it, while the Katherine heir goes without.*

And suddenly the solution presented itself to me, as clearly as a sunburst shining through a cloud-covered sky.

My ball will be canceled, too, I vowed. *If the Katherine heir can't have a ball, then the Elizabeth heir won't have one either.*

3

As soon as the thought hit me, I started to feel better. Canceling my birthday ball wasn't much—it wouldn't save Vandermeer Steel or keep Kay and her family in their home—but it was something that I could *do* to acknowledge that I would always stand by my beloved cousin.

As soon as Madame Lorraine left, Maggie turned down the covers. "Here, milady. I've a fresh nightdress for you," she began.

"Nightdress? Oh, no, Maggie. I don't want to go to bed. I'm not *that* bad off, but listen. I've had an idea. . . ."

She looked at me with wide gray eyes and waited for me to continue.

"I'm going to cancel my birthday ball!" I announced.

Maggie gasped in surprise. "Oh, Lady Betsy! Why would you do such a thing?"

A frown flickered across my face at her response. I'd thought Maggie would understand and tell me it was a wonderful idea, but if anything, she seemed upset. Perhaps I just needed to explain my reasoning to her.

"Well, it's not right. Don't you see?" I continued. "Why should I get to have a ball when Kay doesn't? It isn't fair. Don't you agree?"

Maggie looked troubled. "It's not my place to have an opinion, milady," she replied hesitantly.

"But I have asked you for your opinion!" I reminded her. "Please, tell me what you think!"

"It just seems to me that a birthday ball would be a wonderful thing," Maggie said, a faraway look on her face. "A dream come true, even. Most girls can only dream of something so special. And it makes me sad that you should miss it. You've had a shock, milady—such dreadful news about your cousin. Perhaps . . . if I might be so bold . . . you might not want to be so hasty in your decision. Perhaps you'll reconsider after you've had some time to come to terms with what has happened to your poor cousin and her family."

"I won't reconsider," I said, realizing it was foolish to think that Maggie would understand.

"I'm sure you know best, milady," she replied hesitantly. She looked concerned, as if she sensed my disappointment.

"I'd like to wear my pink dress again," I said, changing the subject. And we didn't say one more word about my ball while Maggie helped me get dressed. After I was ready, Maggie excused herself to see to some mending, leaving me alone with my thoughts. It still seemed like the right decision to cancel the ball, but Maggie's objections had planted a seed of doubt in my mind. Was I being too hasty in my decision? I knew there was someone whose advice I could completely trust: our new chef, Juliette. So I set off for the kitchen.

Juliette had joined the staff at Chatswood Manor only six months ago, but I could hardly remember what life had been like without her. She was from France and so fun and sophisticated; she had traveled halfway around the world as the personal chef for the Countess of Dumoyne. It seemed to me that life in the country would be frightfully dull for Juliette after all her adventures, but she promised me that she loved it here. I hoped she would never leave!

"*Bonjour, ma petite ange!*" Juliette sang out as I entered the kitchen.

"*Bonjour*, Juliette!" I replied. My French accent had improved by leaps and bounds since Juliette and I had started having our little chats.

"Sit, sit," Juliette ordered, pointing at the tiny table and two chairs beneath the window, where we passed many hours telling stories. "Are you hungry? Thirsty? Some tea, I think, and some cakes—as long as you promise not to tell your dear *maman*. She would be very cross with me if I spoiled your appetite for dinner!"

I grinned. "The secret's safe with me," I promised. "But you must be so busy with your preparations for tonight, Juliette. I should hate to get in the way."

"Nonsense!" Juliette declared. "This is the calm before the storm. The roast is in the oven, the soup is simmering, the cakes are cooling—there is nothing more to do until the dinner hour draws closer. I'd love some company to pass the time. Now, sit, and tell me all about the fitting. Did you choose a trim for your gown? Tell me everything!"

Remembering the fitting—and the dreadful news that had interrupted it—wiped the smile from my face.

Juliette could tell at once that something was wrong. "Dear me," she said. "What has happened? Is there a problem with your gown? Are you unhappy with Madame Lorraine's work?"

I shook my head. "Oh, no, Juliette. It's ever so much worse than that," I replied glumly. Then I told her about the terrible plight that had befallen my American relations.

Juliette sucked in her breath sharply and reached across the table. "I am so very sorry to hear this, Lady Betsy," she said gravely as she patted my hand. "It has come as a terrible shock, I'm sure. I can see how heavily it weighs upon you."

"It's so wrong," I tried to explain. "My cousin Kay is the kindest, sweetest girl I know. And now her whole life is turned upside down. I feel so helpless, and I want to do something to help. I know this sounds rather impulsive, but I think I have made a decision. I'm just not sure whether it's a wise decision or not."

"Go on. Go on," Juliette said encouragingly. "Tell me what you are thinking."

"I want to cancel my ball," I finally said. "It seems unfair to spend so much time and money on a lavish party while Kay and her parents are on the verge of losing everything—their business, their fortune, their *home.*"

For a moment, Juliette stared at me without speaking. *Oh, no,* I thought. *It really is a terrible idea. She's going to say the same thing as Maggie. Doesn't* anybody *see it my way?*

Then, to my surprise, Juliette leaned across the table and kissed me quickly on each cheek.

"I beg your pardon, Lady Betsy," she said at once. "I am so moved by your good and generous heart—my emotions have gotten the better of me."

A faint blush crept into my cheeks, but if Juliette noticed, she didn't let on.

"So many gestures are, at their core, empty," she continued, waving her hand in the air. "But *this*, Lady Betsy, *this* is not just grand, but also *noble.*"

"Maggie thought I was being too hasty. She said it made her sad to think of me canceling my ball."

Juliette sniffed contemptuously. "Maggie! What does she know? I have heard that . . . well, never mind."

"What have you heard?" I asked.

"I shouldn't tell you this, Lady Betsy, but the

housemaids think her a fool and utterly unsuited for the role," Juliette confided in a loud whisper. "Oh, I felt so bad for you when I heard them say it! You deserve the best lady's maid in the world, not some nincompoop who should be milking cows in a barn."

"She's not that bad—" I started to say. But Juliette kept speaking very fast.

"Have you spoken to your mother about canceling the ball?"

"Not yet," I replied. "She's been poring over her ledgers since the phone call with Aunt Kate. There was something else from the phone call that she wouldn't tell me."

"Really?" Juliette asked, sitting a little straighter. "What could that be?"

"I have no idea. But she wouldn't say a word."

"This is so strange to me," Juliette said, shaking her head. "In my family, we keep no secrets. Even the bad things, we tell one another."

"You think it's something bad?" I asked anxiously. How could it be any worse than what Mum had already confided?

Juliette opened her mouth to speak, then closed it

as if she had changed her mind. "It would not be my place to say, Lady Betsy," she finally replied. "But I do think that you should speak to your mother at once about canceling the ball."

"Right now?" I said. "But the advisers—"

"Are not due until three o'clock. So I believe you will have just enough time to make your case."

"All right," I said.

"And you must tell me right away what she says," Juliette said as she began to clear the table. "Do you promise to tell me everything?"

"Of course," I said. "Wish me luck!"

"*Bonne chance!*" Juliette replied, her eyes twinkling. "Not that you'll need it!"

I hurried upstairs to the library, where I guessed Mum would still be reviewing the accounts. I was right; I found her sitting at the desk, poring over a thick ledger.

"Mum?" I said.

She looked up and smiled at me before gazing back at the accounts laid out before her. "Hello, Betsy. All done with your fitting?"

"Yes," I replied. "Well, actually, no, I suppose. I—I didn't feel up to it. Not after . . ."

Mum nodded sympathetically. "I understand, my dear. I know that after I got off the phone with Kate, I was certainly too preoccupied to pay much attention to anything. Now, did you tell Madame Lorraine when to return? I know it seems like a month is a very long time, but for the amount of work she has to do to finish your gown, there really is no time to spare."

"That's the thing," I began. Then I took a deep breath and searched for the right words before I continued. Mum could tell that I had something important to say; she closed her ledger, pushed it across her desk, and gave me her full attention.

"I think we should cancel my birthday ball," I said.

Mum's face stayed blank; I couldn't begin to guess what she thought. "Go on."

One by one, I told Mum all my reasons.

"You make some very good points," she said slowly. Her index finger tapped the sapphires of the Elizabeth necklace, like she always did when she was deep in thought. "But, Betsy, you've been dreaming of your twelfth birthday ball for your whole life. I remember all too well what that was like; it's not so very long ago that I was twelve myself, you know. At least, it doesn't feel so long ago.

"I can appreciate your thinking, Betsy, and it is very admirable for you to want to do something so selfless. But you must consider this choice very carefully. This would be the very first time in the history of the Chatswood family without a grand ball to celebrate a girl's twelfth birthday. I don't want you to make your decision in haste and regret it later."

"I won't regret it," I said firmly. "It seems wrong for the Elizabeth heir to have a birthday ball while the Katherine heir goes without. I'd like to . . . to find another way to celebrate. Something that Kay could do as well. Perhaps instead of spending all that money on a big party for only me, we can think of a way to put the money toward something to celebrate both of us, as a family. I think that's what Great-Great-Grandmother Elizabeth would have wanted. What do you think, Mum?"

"I think that's a splendid idea," Mum replied, a proud smile breaking over her face.

My heart leaped. "So you agree?" I asked excitedly. "We should cancel?"

"If and *only* if it's what you truly want."

"It is."

"Then that's what we will do," Mum replied, holding up her palms.

"Oh, thank you, Mum! Thank you!" I cried as I hugged her.

"And your timing is perfect, Betsy, because when the advisers arrive this afternoon, we'll revise the accounts accordingly," Mum continued. "Starting tomorrow, you and I shall begin the work of undoing the preparations we've already made."

"Thank you again," I said, feeling at a loss for words and overwhelmed with love for my mum. I knew I had made the right decision, and my heart swelled knowing how much trust Mum was placing in me.

Just then, a loud chime rang through the room.

Mum rose from her desk. "The advisers are here," she said. "Run along now, Betsy, and I'll see you at dinner."

"Yes, Mum," I said.

Remembering my promise to Juliette, I returned to the kitchen right away. She and her assistant, Eloise, were piping delicate rosettes of frosting onto a layer cake.

"She agreed to cancel!" I cried happily, raising my voice over the clanging from the back of the kitchen, where Daphne, the scullery maid, was scouring copper pots. "My birthday ball is canceled!"

Eloise was so shocked that she dropped her spatula, splattering frosting across the tiles. "My apologies," she murmured as she bent down to wipe up the mess with a rag.

But Juliette grinned at me from behind her pastry bag. "Oh, wonderful," she said, sounding genuinely pleased. "I'm really not surprised. Canceling the ball will save your mother a tremendous amount of money. I am sure that Lady Beth is very grateful for your decision."

My smile faltered. "What—what do you mean?"

"Oh, dear. Now I've upset you!" she cried. "Lady Betsy, you must not pay any attention to me."

"Do you think there's a problem with our estate's finances?" I asked anxiously.

Juliette bent so low over the cake that I couldn't see her face. "Many estates are overburdened by debt," she said. "But I am just the chef. I wouldn't know about such things."

"But it sounded a moment ago like you knew something," I said. "Please, if you know something, do tell me!"

"Of course I do not know anything. As I said, I wouldn't know about such things," Juliette responded. But I had the feeling she wasn't telling me something. Or that she was afraid to tell me something. A knot formed in my stomach as I tried to think of a way to convince Juliette to tell me what she knew.

"Eloise!" Juliette exclaimed suddenly. "What happened to your pastry bag?"

In her haste to clean up the spilled frosting, Eloise had left her pastry bag unattended, and a large pool of frosting had oozed out of it.

"Daphne! Please bring some wet rags and help Eloise clean this mess at once. I can't stand an untidy kitchen," Juliette said. Then she turned to me with an apologetic smile. "You must excuse us, Lady Betsy," she continued. "We are so eager to make a good impression on the council of advisers tonight. It's of the utmost importance that they view Chatswood Manor as a model of efficiency and frugality, you know."

"Yes, of course," I said. I knew now wasn't the time

to try to get more information out of Juliette. She had an important job to do, and I didn't want to be in the way. "Thank you for listening, Juliette. The cake looks beautiful."

"You are too kind," she replied. Then she turned back to the cake, adding a cascade of rosettes to the top tier. I wished that I had something equally engrossing to capture my attention. Because try as I might, I couldn't forget Juliette's words: *Canceling the ball will save your mother a tremendous amount of money.*

Was it possible that Mum and I were in the same situation as our American relations?

4

Dear Cousin Kay,

Mum told me of the terrible trials facing you. Oh, Kay, I am so sorry! I want you to know that I love you so much and I wish that there was some way for me to help. Please tell me if there is anything I can do! Today I made the decision to cancel my birthday ball. I know it's not much, but I won't have one if you can't.

I was interrupted by Maggie's knock at the door; it was time to get ready for dinner. She helped me put on my best dress and brushed my hair until it shone brighter than a bronze penny. Maggie had just finished pulling my hair back with a rhinestone barrette when Nellie came to fetch me.

"All ready, Lady Betsy?" she asked. "You look pretty as a picture! Come along, now. Everyone's in the drawing room. Mr. Embry will announce dinner shortly."

"Thank you, Nellie," I replied.

As we walked to the drawing room, I noticed that Nellie was unusually quiet. "Any news from the tour?" I asked. Whenever the advisers visited, they spent hours locked in the library with Mum, poring over the accounts; afterward, Mum took them on a tour of the grounds so that they could see how the estate fared. Mum and her council of advisers didn't always see eye to eye, but that had never stopped Mum from voicing her opinions.

"Ah, well, that's not for me to say, milady," Nellie said in such a way that I could tell she knew more than she was willing to let on. But before I could ask what she meant, we had reached the drawing room, and Nellie gave me a quick smile before retreating down the corridor.

"Excellent timing, Lady Betsy," a deep voice murmured behind me.

I turned around to see our butler, Mr. Embry.

"Is it time for dinner already?" I asked as he reached past me to open the door.

"Indeed it is, and I think you'll be highly pleased with the meal," he replied.

I smiled to myself as I remembered the delectable cake that Juliette had labored over.

"Darling!" Mum cried when she saw me standing in the doorway. "Do come in. We were just talking about you!" She turned to the three gentlemen standing beside her, who bowed as I approached. I remembered them well, of course: Lord Turley with his sharply pointed beard; Mr. Markham with his shiny silver hair; and Mr. Edwards, who had a perfectly round pair of spectacles perched upon the bridge of his nose. They had been Papa's dearest friends before he died, and it was in honor of his memory that they took such an interest in Chatswood Manor, offering Mum their guidance and expertise as she managed the estate and family fortune.

As usual, the council's wives had arrived to join us for dinner. Mrs. Markham was my favorite. Her blue eyes flashed merrily at me as she took my hands. "My dear Lady Beth, you must be mistaken," Mrs. Markham said to Mum. "Betsy is but a child, not a sophisticated young lady like I see before me."

I smiled as I curtsied to her. Mrs. Markham was known for exaggeration, but the compliment made me happy all the same.

"Dinner is served," Mr. Embry announced in his most somber voice.

I followed the group into the dining room and, when everyone was ready to be seated, took my place on Mum's right side. The footmen had scarcely begun to serve the first course when Lord Turley turned toward me.

"Now, now," he began in his gruff voice. "What's this nonsense I hear about canceling your birthday ball, young lady?"

A warning flashed through Mum's eyes—but it wasn't directed at me.

"Lord Turley, I thought that this matter was settled," she began, but a cry from Lady Turley interrupted her.

"You must be joking, Thomas!" she exclaimed. "Canceling the birthday ball? Why, I've never heard of such a thing!"

"Oh, you mustn't," implored Mrs. Edwards. "I ordered my gown months ago!"

"You see?" Lord Turley said triumphantly. "Surely you'll reconsider this foolishness. Why, I've never known a girl your age who wasn't utterly delighted by the notion of a ball in her honor. What possible reason could you have to cancel?"

I was about to explain about my cousin Kay's situation when Mum spoke for me.

"We're so sorry to disappoint you," Mother said with a steady voice. "But I can assure you that Betsy and I have given the matter careful thought and remain confident that we've reached the right decision."

"Right for whom?" challenged Lord Turley. "Certainly not for the estate. Why, when word gets out, the rumors will be scandalous, to say the least."

"Rumors," Mum replied, shaking her head contemptuously. "I've never given much mind to such things, and I know that you haven't either, Lord Turley."

"What *seems to be* is as important as *what is*," Mr. Edwards said. He fancied himself very wise, but often his words left me confused. "You must ask yourselves if this is the message you want to send to the county: that

Chatswood Manor can no longer manage to maintain the oldest traditions of the family."

"But that's not why we canceled!" I exclaimed. I snuck a glance at Mum out of the corner of my eye as I suddenly wondered . . . *or is it?*

"Of course not," Mum said firmly. "And really, Mr. Edwards, I believe you are leaping to conclusions. You reviewed the accounts yourself just this afternoon. The estate is sound. How could anyone suspect that we canceled the ball due to financial troubles?"

"Perhaps anyone who *hasn't* reviewed the accounts," Mr. Markham said darkly. "Or any garden-variety gossipmonger, of which our community boasts many, I'm sorry to say."

"I'm not about to let the fear of such people dictate my decisions," Mum replied.

"There has been talk, though," Mr. Markham continued. "My valet mentioned that—"

"*Surely*, Mr. Markham, you wouldn't bring baseless gossip to my table!" Mum exclaimed, her eyes wide with astonishment.

Mr. Markham flushed with embarrassment, but before he could continue, Lord Turley spoke up. "If the ball must be canceled, I can't understand why the money you allocated for it won't be returned to the general account."

"Because that money still belongs to Betsy—to celebrate her birthday as she and I see fit," Mum explained. "And that is my final word on the subject."

"I *do* wish you would reconsider," Mrs. Edwards said with a pout. "I was very much looking forward to debuting my new gown."

"We are sorry," Mum apologized again, "but I'm afraid that we cannot be swayed. Now, Mr. Edwards, you must promise me that you will take your beautiful wife to London this spring. I should hate to think of her new gown languishing in the wardrobe, unworn!"

Then Mum laughed; the sound was so lilting and lovely that she never laughed alone. Soon even Lord Turley was smiling. I laughed, too, but it wasn't genuine. I would've given *anything* to know what Mr. Markham's valet had told him. What was the nature of these rumors . . . and who was spreading them?

And perhaps most important, why was Mum so quick to silence them?

A few days later, I spent my afternoon writing beside Mum in the library. The decision to cancel my ball wasn't difficult, but undoing the preparations we'd made turned out to be much more complicated. Mum had telephoned the vendors right away to cancel, but she said that I had to write personal notes to everyone who'd been invited. Every day, I wrote so many notes that by dinnertime, my numb fingers could barely hold a pen. Worst of all, I had barely even begun my letter to Kay!

I was laboring over a note to the Honorable Lord and Lady Lorrington when Mum glanced at my work. A slight frown crossed her face. "Be mindful of your penmanship, Betsy," she said gently. "Beautiful words deserve beautiful handwriting."

"My handwriting would be more beautiful if my hand didn't feel like it was about to fall off!" I complained as I put down my pen and shook my fingers. "I wish I had a typewriter."

Mum looked shocked. "A typewriter! Betsy, you can't write a note on a typewriter. It's too impersonal."

"I think it looks smart," I replied. "So professional! My *Hollywood Hello* magazine had a page from a real radio play script, and it was done on a typewriter. If I had one, I might try writing a radio pl—"

I was interrupted by Mr. Embry as he delivered the afternoon post.

"No telegrams today?" Mum asked.

"I'm afraid not, milady."

"I see. Thank you, Mr. Embry," Mum said as she flipped through the letters. "Oh, look, Betsy. Here's one from my cousin Gabrielle in Paris. She must've written a response the moment she received your note."

What had I written to Cousin Gabrielle? I tried to remember, but all the notes I'd written over the past few days were a blur.

"Shall I read it aloud?" Mum asked. "'Dearest Beth, I was ever so pleased to receive a note from little Betsy, especially since I have long desired to know her better. Then I opened the letter and read its contents. To say that I am astonished would be an understatement! I cannot believe that the birthday ball has been canceled. It is unthinkable—unspeakable—unbearable—'"

Mum looked at me with her eyes twinkling. "It goes on like that for quite a while," she said. "Shall I skip ahead?"

"Yes, please," I said. Mum remained good-spirited about everything, but I'd grown tired of hearing how much I'd shocked everyone.

Mum's eyes darted back and forth as she scanned the letter. Suddenly, they grew wide. "And so I write to inform you that you should expect me as planned. Even without the grand birthday ball, I am certain that Betsy's birthday will be a memorable occasion and I would not miss it for anything. In addition, I have sent word to Madame Lorraine that she is *not* relieved of her duties; instead, I have commissioned two additional gowns from her, one for you, Beth, and one for me as well! We shall be the most stylish ladies in all of England when she is done!"

"*What* did you say?" I exclaimed. "Cousin Gabrielle is coming anyway?"

"It appears so," Mum replied.

I could hardly hide my surprise. Mum and Gabrielle weren't that close; in fact, I'd met Gabrielle only once, and I was so young at the time that I couldn't even remember her. But I'd heard all about her, and the stories were . . . well, they were outrageous! She'd come to England twenty years ago for Mum's twelfth birthday ball and had caused quite a scandal when she tried to frame Mum's lady's maid, Shannon, for theft. Luckily, Mum had figured out the truth just in time to save Shannon from being sacked, and Gabrielle had gone home to Paris in disgrace. According to Mum, Gabrielle had apologized and seen the error of her ways, but I was still troubled by what she had done all those years ago. What if she hadn't really changed her ways? The more I thought about it, the more I realized that I didn't want to spend my birthday with her now that our American relatives couldn't join us. It was one thing when she was coming along with our other relatives, but another thing to think of spending time with just her. But from Gabrielle's letter, it sounded like I didn't have a choice.

"Mr. Embry, would you please send for Juliette?" Mum was saying. When our housekeeper had retired a few months ago, Mum had decided not to replace her, choosing instead to give orders directly to the staff.

"Certainly, milady," he replied, bowing before he left the library.

"Oh, Mum, must Cousin Gabrielle come?" I asked. "After we canceled the ball, I'd thought it would be just you and me on my birthday—"

"That's what I'd thought, too," Mum replied. "But Gabrielle is family, Betsy. I don't see how I could possibly ask her to stay home. Especially after she's gone to so much trouble to arrange for Madame Lorraine."

Before I could answer, Juliette arrived. She flashed me a very quick smile as she stepped into the library, then turned all her attention to Mum. "May I help you, milady?"

"Yes, Juliette, thank you," Mum told her. "Our cousin Gabrielle will be joining us next week, and she's written with some very specific food requests."

Mum held out a page from Gabrielle's letter. As Juliette glanced at it, I noticed all the color drain from her face. *Poor Juliette,* I thought. *Whatever Gabrielle wants must be especially complicated. Why should she have to go to so much extra trouble just to please Gabrielle?*

"As a courtesy to our guest, I'd like to make sure she's happy," Mum continued. "So please take whatever steps necessary to fulfill these requests."

"Of course, milady," Juliette replied. "It will be my pleasure."

"Thank you, Juliette," Mum said as she returned to her stack of letters.

Juliette curtsied before she hurried from the room. But she still looked more worried than I'd ever seen her before.

"What was on that list?" I asked curiously.

"Let's see . . . rack of lamb with mint sauce, crêpe suzette, and lobster thermidor, among others," Mum replied. "Cousin Gabrielle has always had very particular tastes."

And a distinct lack of manners, I thought.

Mum spoke up, as if she knew what I was thinking. "She can be quite charming. Gabrielle's really the life of the party, you know. I suspect you'll enjoy her company more than you think. I have no doubt that your birthday will be infinitely more exciting with Gabrielle at Chatswood Manor."

I hoped Mum was right . . . but I still wasn't convinced.

After I finished my notes, I went to the kitchen to see Juliette.

"Ah, Lady Betsy!" she said with a warm smile. "I am glad to see you!"

"Is everything all right?" I asked. "You looked so worried in the library—"

Juliette quickly shook her head. "Oh, you must pay me no mind, milady," she replied. "It is true that your cousin's requests are . . . somewhat surprising. To be truthful, I'm still not accustomed to taking orders directly from the lady of the house. Ever since Mrs. Murphy was let go, it has been difficult for me to adjust, but I must do my best."

"Mrs. Murphy wasn't let go," I corrected Juliette. "She wanted to retire."

"Oh. Did she?" Juliette asked. "That's not what I heard. I thought your mother sacked her to save on the expense of her salary—"

"That's not true!" I cried. "Mum would never do such a thing!"

"Yes, I am sure you are right," Juliette said right away. "I am so sorry, Lady Betsy. I must remember not to believe everything I hear. Besides, everyone knows that Lady Beth is a good and kind woman."

"Yes, she is," I said. I took a deep breath and tried to calm myself down. I shouldn't get upset at Juliette, I realized—she was just telling me what she had heard. I knew she meant no harm. The real reason I was upset was Cousin Gabrielle. "I can hardly believe that Mum and Gabrielle are cousins," I said to Juliette, changing the subject. "Do you know what Gabrielle did when she visited Chatswood for Mum's birthday? She was jealous of Mum receiving the Elizabeth necklace, so Gabrielle ordered her lady's maid to throw away her own heirloom necklace in hopes that she'd get a fancier one to replace it. Then she tried to blame Mum's lady's maid for stealing it—when really her own lady's maid was to blame!"

"She sounds like a *monster*," Juliette replied. "I hope she doesn't try to ruin your birthday like she ruined your mother's."

"I hope not as well," I echoed. But if Cousin Gabrielle had more mischief in mind, would there be any way to stop her?

5

The next morning I was continuing my letter to Kay when Mum stopped by my room. "It's such a beautiful day, Betsy," she said. "Would you like to take a walk in the garden with me?"

"Of course!" I replied, putting down my pen at once.

"Oh, good," Mum said, linking her arm through mine. "I've been so busy lately, I feel as though I've barely seen you. And there's something that I've been wanting to talk with you about."

My pulse quickened. *Could this be the big secret?* I wondered. "What's that?"

"Let's discuss it in the garden," Mum replied.

We had nearly reached the front door when Mr. Embry hurried up to us.

"Lady Beth—" he began.

"Good morning, Mr. Embry," Mum said. "Betsy

and I are off for a walk in the garden. But before we go, have there been any telegrams?"

Mr. Embry shook his head as he tried to catch his breath. "No, milady, not today," he replied. "However, you have just now received some visitors. They are in the drawing room."

"Visitors!" Mum repeated in surprise. "I wasn't expecting anyone. Who is it, Mr. Embry?"

"Your advisory council, milady."

Mum looked puzzled. "That's odd," she said. "They were here just last week." Then she turned to me. "I'm so sorry, Betsy, but we'll have to take our walk another time."

"I understand," I said, trying to hide my disappointment.

"I knew you would." Mum leaned forward to kiss my cheek, then disappeared down the corridor with Mr. Embry.

What am I going to do now? I thought. I could've gone back to my room and written to Kay, but how could I concentrate on my letter knowing that Mum wanted to tell me something important? Wondering what the big secret could be had been on my mind for months. If I didn't find out soon, I might burst!

Mum has been so preoccupied with her correspondence lately, I thought, remembering all the letters she'd received and her constant checking for a telegram. Maybe the answers to my questions were lurking in one of those letters. Maybe if I took a peek at Mum's desk, the secret would reveal itself to me!

It's no harm to look, I told myself as I set off for the library. *Mum always says that learning how to manage Chatswood is my responsibility and my duty. She would be proud of my initiative!*

But even as I thought those things, I found myself walking very quickly, and very quietly, hoping that no one would see me. And I would've made it, too—if I hadn't collided with Juliette the moment I entered the library!

"Ow!" I cried.

"Lady Betsy!" Juliette exclaimed. "I am so sorry! Oh, I *am* clumsy—are you all right?"

"Yes, yes, I'm fine," I said, rubbing a sore spot on my head. "I'm so surprised to see you here. Are *you* all right?"

"I am fine, milady, and thank you for asking."

"Mum's in the drawing room," I said. "Did you need her? Her advisers dropped by unexpectedly."

"I was just . . . I wanted to deliver the grocer's bill," Juliette explained, gesturing to Mum's desk. I glanced over and noticed how untidy it appeared, cluttered with loose papers. "The monthly payment is quite overdue, so I—"

"Overdue?" I repeated.

"Surely nothing to worry about," said Juliette. "Lady Beth is a very busy woman. No doubt trivialities like bills can easily slip her mind."

"But Mum always keeps the accounts current," I said, confused. "She prides herself on it."

"Of course she does!" Juliette said. "That's why I wanted to make sure that I, personally, brought the bill to her. Now, if you'll excuse me, Lady Betsy, I must go back to the kitchen. The preparations for Lady Gabrielle's visit are wearing me to the bone."

"I'm sorry, Juliette. You already work so hard."

"It's no trouble, really," she said. "As long as all Lady Gabrielle does is make demands of me, all shall be well. My real concern is that . . . Oh, never mind that."

"What is it?" I asked.

Juliette looked troubled. "I just hate to think that Lady Gabrielle has plans to run through your mother's fortune as she's already run through her own."

"What?" I gasped in shock.

"I thought you knew," Juliette said, lowering her voice to a whisper. She glanced around to make sure no one was listening. "The rumor is that Gabrielle is quite destitute. Penniless, really, and subsisting on the charity of friends and relations."

"I had *no* idea!"

"Isn't that why the advisers are here today?"

"I—I don't know," I stammered.

"I can't imagine why else they'd come so soon after their last visit," Juliette told me. "But it's none of my business, Lady Betsy. You mustn't say anything to your mother about this conversation. Now, if you'll excuse me—"

"Of course," I replied. I gave her hand a grateful squeeze. "And *thank you* for telling me, Juliette."

"It's your fortune, too, you know," she told me in a somber voice. "You have a right to know."

Then Juliette hurried toward the kitchen.

I immediately set off for the drawing room. It wouldn't be right to burst in on Mum's meeting uninvited, but I wanted to hear the advisers' concerns for myself.

I agree with Juliette, I thought in determination. *I* do *have a right to know.*

The drawing-room doors were closed, but Mum and the advisers were speaking at full volume. I could hear every word.

"Our concerns are *not* unfounded." That had to be Lord Turley. "If it is true that Lady Gabrielle has fallen on reduced circumstances—"

"Which it is *not,*" Mum said angrily.

"Then we have a duty and an obligation to the estate to ensure that its fortunes will stay intact," he continued.

Mr. Markham spoke up. "The word is that she would like to ask you for a sizable loan. Which is not out of the question—"

"I should say that it is!" argued Mr. Edwards.

"Which is not out of the question if there is some sort of collateral attached," Mr. Markham continued. "But to verify such a thing, we would need to send a representative to Paris to examine her accounts."

"This conversation is an outrage," Mum said. "Have you forgotten that you are speaking of Lady Gabrielle Trufant, my own blood relation, in my home?"

There was a long, uncomfortable silence.

"Perhaps you would be more willing to discuss this other issue," Lord Turley said. I heard the rustle of papers.

"Exactly what are you asking?" Mum replied, her voice like ice.

"You have withdrawn a large sum of money from the general account," said Lord Turley. "I would like to inquire why."

"And I would like to remind you that that is none of your business," Mum said. "Your conservatorship does not extend to my personal use of my—"

"Lady Betsy!"

It was Maggie! And she looked horrified to discover me listening at the door!

"Come away from there," she said in a low voice. "You haven't got the right to eavesdrop—"

"I do!" I yelled, wrenching my arm away from her—and completely forgetting to keep my voice down. "*You* haven't got the right to tell me what to do!"

There was a sudden silence in the drawing room. I was filled with dread as I realized just how loudly I'd spoken. I heard footsteps, the door swung open, and there stood Mum, looking angrier than I'd ever seen her.

"Betsy!" she exclaimed. "Were you listening at the door?"

I stared into my mother's eyes and knew that I had to tell the truth. "I—I—I—" But somehow, I couldn't bring myself to say the words.

"I have never been so disappointed in you," Mum said. "Maggie, please take Betsy to her room and stay with her until I've concluded my meeting."

Then, without another word, Mum turned around, closing the door behind her.

In the end, there was nothing the advisers could say or do that would change Mum's mind about Gabrielle's visit. A week later I stood in the grand hall next to Mum while we waited for our chauffeur, Lionel, to return with Gabrielle from the train station. I glanced at Mum out of the corner of my eye. After giving me a short lecture on respecting the privacy of closed doors, she hadn't said another word about my eavesdropping. But I couldn't shake the feeling that she was unhappy with me. Mum was so busy every day that I scarcely saw her, and when I did, she seemed unusually preoccupied. Even now, in the hallway, there was a tightness around her mouth, and her forehead was wrinkled as if something was troubling her.

"We never did take our walk," Mum said suddenly. "I'm sorry, Betsy. It completely slipped my mind."

"That's all right."

"I asked Juliette to prepare a light luncheon, and the footmen have set up a table in the garden, among the peonies," Mum continued. "It will be a lovely way to get reacquainted with Cousin Gabrielle."

She looked so worried, staring off into the distance, that I wanted to ask her what was wrong. But before I could, we heard the motorcar arrive. In an instant, all Mum's worries seemed to melt away as a beaming smile transformed her face. I followed her quick footsteps outside just as Cousin Gabrielle stepped out of the motorcar.

I didn't remember Gabrielle from her last visit,

which had happened more than ten years ago. I wasn't quite sure what I had expected . . . but certainly not this!

Gabrielle's lemon-yellow hair was slicked back in a glossy bob. Enormous diamond chandelier earrings dangled beside her cheeks, scattering flashes of light across her rouged face. Even her lips were painted as red as a toffee apple from the fair! There was a fur stole wrapped around her shoulders despite the warmth of the day. She looked like she had stepped out of *Hollywood Hello* magazine.

"Welcome, dear Gabrielle!" Mum exclaimed, reaching out her hands.

"Cousin Beth," Gabrielle cried, swooping toward Mum and wrapping her in a hug. "It has been too long!"

"Far too long," Mum agreed.

Gabrielle stepped back and held Mum at arm's length, eyeing her carefully. "You are looking well," she finally declared. "But tired. And—ah, ah, ah, what is this I see? Wrinkles?"

"Laugh lines," Mum protested, ducking away from Gabrielle's grasp.

"No, no, no. There is nothing funny about them," Gabrielle retorted. "You are too young for such things. You worry too much, I think. Never mind. I am here now, and I will take care of *everything*."

"Really," Mum said, "such things do not concern me!"

"Oh, but they should!" Gabrielle exclaimed. "I will send to my personal chemist in Paris for a wonderful new cream for your face," Gabrielle promised. "It is no trouble at all. You will love it, Beth. You will look ten years younger!"

"Betsy!" Mum called to me. "Come here, darling, and say hello to Cousin Gabrielle!"

I took a deep breath and stepped forward. As Gabrielle rushed forward to hug me, I braced my shoulders—and a good thing, too, because I think she would've knocked me right over!

"Betsy, Betsy, Betsy!" Gabrielle cried. "Look how you've grown. Oh, I knew you would be beautiful, but no, it is not possible that you have become *such* a beauty. My goodness!"

"Thank y—"

"But I will *never* understand why you canceled your ball." Gabrielle spoke right over me, then turned to Mum. "Or why *you* let her. A Chatswood family *tradition*—"

"Adam! William!" Mum called to our footmen. "Would you please bring Lady Gabrielle's luggage to the guest suite?"

"This is my lady's maid, Bernadette," Gabrielle said, snapping her fingers at a young woman who was thin as a reed and looked meeker than a mouse. "*Go*, Bernadette, and unpack my gowns. I'll want the crimson one for dinner, so make sure that it's ready. Go!"

Bernadette rushed after the footmen, who were struggling under the weight of an enormous steamer trunk. Then, to my astonishment, I realized that Gabrielle had brought *three* more trunks as well! *How can one person need so much luggage?* I wondered. *Exactly how long is Cousin Gabrielle planning to stay?*

"You must be in need of some refreshment," Mum was saying. "I've arranged for a light luncheon in the garden—"

"No, not at all, but do send for Madame Lorraine," Gabrielle interrupted her. "I telegraphed her last week that she should begin sketching designs for my new gown, and I can't wait to see them! You'll see, Beth, the good a new gown can do for a woman. You look sorely in need of one yourself."

Then she linked arms with Mum and started up the stairs, leaving me standing outside, all alone. It was like they'd both forgotten all about me—even Mum, who seemed completely happy to be with her cousin. Happier than she'd been in weeks. I loved seeing my mum so happy, but I couldn't help remembering what I had heard the advisers say about Gabrielle. What if she was laying a trap for Mum, and Mum was walking right into it?

I was more determined than ever to keep my wits about me at all times when I was around Cousin Gabrielle. After all, I had to look out for my mum.

6

Later that day, I continued my letter to Kay.

Cousin Gabrielle arrived this morning, Kay. I don't know how to say this, but . . . she's even worse than I expected! Loud and brash, she talks over everyone else and seems content only when she is the center of attention. Madame Lorraine brought over her sketches for Gabrielle and Mum's new gowns, and Gabrielle's is the most ostentatious dress I've ever seen, with real ostrich plumes sewn into the skirt. Mum's is much more dignified. And the oddest thing of all is that Mum actually seems to enjoy having Gabrielle here!

It seems so fundamentally unfair that Gabrielle is visiting us and not you, Kay. I would give anything to have you here in her place.

I paused in my writing and frowned at the page. *Would reading this upset Kay?* I wondered. *It's got to be just as hard on her to be staying home. I'd hate to send her a letter that makes her feel even worse about everything*

I crumpled up the page and tossed it into the wastebasket, feeling an immense ache of loneliness. I wanted so badly to *talk* to someone about my concerns—like Kay or Mum or even my former lady's maid, Emily. But Kay was unreachable; Emily was gone; and Mum . . . well, I couldn't talk to Mum, not the way I wanted to, not with Gabrielle taking up all her time. I realized that this was the very first time in my whole life when I hadn't been able to go to Mum with my troubles. And that made me feel even sadder.

Juliette! I suddenly thought. *Juliette will understand!*

I found her in the kitchen, dressing a pair of plump

chickens to roast above a bed of carrots, pearl onions, and new potatoes.

"Betsy!" Juliette said, looking genuinely pleased to see me. "I didn't expect to see you, not with your cousin's arrival."

"Am I interrupting?"

"Interrupting? The glamorous life of a chef?" Juliette laughed as she gestured to the trussed-up chickens. "Not at all. Eloise! Please bring Lady Betsy some biscuits and a glass of lemonade."

"Lemonade!" I exclaimed in surprise. "Really? We haven't had lemonade since last summer."

"Yes. I made a large pitcher to serve with dinner tonight. The lemons were dreadfully expensive, but I suppose what Lady Gabrielle wants, Lady Gabrielle shall get."

"Oh, Juliette." I groaned. "She's awful. Dreadful. Worse than ever I dreamed."

Juliette bit her lip. "I—" Then she shook her head. "No. I shouldn't speak of it."

"Speak of what?" I asked. "Did something happen?"

"It was my own fault, really," Juliette said, her eyes sparkling as if they were full of tears. She quickly looked down, staring at her hands. "I'd gone upstairs to . . ."

"Go on," I encouraged her.

"Lady Gabrielle saw me in the corridor and berated me for going upstairs," Juliette said in a hoarse whisper. "Never—in all my years of service—has anyone ever spoken to me like that. She said that the specter of me in my apron was a blemish on the estate—"

"She did *not*!" I gasped in shock.

"And that I'd best remember my place, or I'd find there was no place for me at Chatswood after all."

"She can't do that," I said hotly. "Gabrielle is a *guest* here. She is not in charge of Chatswood Manor."

"Yes, but she has your mother's ear," Juliette said sorrowfully. "I heard that they were laughing together like schoolgirls during their fitting with Madame Lorraine."

I opened my mouth, then closed it when I realized I had nothing to say. It was true that Mum and Gabrielle seemed much chummier than I had expected. But surely Mum would never dismiss Juliette just because Gabrielle told her to!

Or would she?

"Lady Betsy, I've no right to ask, I know," Juliette continued shyly. "But . . . will you help me? I've got to stay out of Lady Gabrielle's way if I'm to keep my position here. And I would hate to leave Chatswood Manor, especially in disgrace if I were sacked."

"You have my word," I promised. "Whatever I can do to help, I will."

"Thank you so much," Juliette replied. "With someone like Lady Gabrielle, I think that 'out of sight, out of mind' is the only way to survive."

"Well, I doubt she's the type to come down to the kitchen," I said. "She'll probably just send messages through her lady's maid. So as long as you stay here—"

"Lady Betsy."

I glanced behind me to see my own lady's maid. "Maggie! What are you doing here?"

"Lady Beth sent me with a request for tea for herself and Lady Gabrielle," Maggie said. Her eyes didn't leave Juliette.

"Of course," Juliette said with a curt nod. "Eloise, a tea service for two. At once."

"Lady Betsy, I suppose you'd best come with me," Maggie said.

"Why?" I protested. "It's not nearly time to dress for dinner."

"I'm in need of your assistance," Maggie pressed. "The charity drive is coming up, and your mother has requested that you donate any gowns and accessories that you no longer want."

"But does it have to be done *right now*?" I argued.

"I'll need to launder everything before I pack it," Maggie said in a small but firm voice.

Realizing that she wasn't going to budge, I sighed heavily and rose from my chair. "I'll see you later, Juliette."

"Whenever you want, milady," she replied. "I am always at your service."

Maggie and I didn't speak as we walked toward the room. *Why can't I have a lady's maid more like Nellie?* I wondered. *Or Juliette!*

Just about *anyone* would be better than Maggie.

After finishing with Maggie as quickly as I could, I went to look for Mum. I found her in the drawing room about to sit down to tea with Gabrielle. Their fitting with Madame Lorraine must've been great fun, because they were still in high spirits when I joined them.

"Betsy! Come sit," Mum called when she saw me hovering in the doorway.

I was barely seated before a footman had quickly added another place setting to the table. William wheeled in the tea cart, which was laden with platters of dainty sandwiches, iced cakes, and delicate biscuits.

"Cousin Gabrielle's had an idea," Mum said. "Go ahead, Gabrielle. Tell her."

"Your mother tells me that neither of you know the American dances," Gabrielle announced. "Disgraceful! No wonder you canceled your ball. After dinner, I will teach you the jitterbug, the fox-trot, the Lindy hop, everything!"

"But my radio program is on tonight," I reminded Mum. "I don't want to miss it."

She frowned slightly. "You can catch it next week. I think dancing lessons from Gabrielle will be fun."

"And tomorrow Bernadette will cut your hair," Gabrielle told me. "I think a bob would be darling on you, just darling! You will look just like me!"

I looked at Mum in alarm. I *loved* my long hair!

But before I could protest, Mr. Embry entered the drawing room. His face was as red as a bowl of beets.

"Lady Beth," he said in a low voice. "If I might have a word."

"Certainly, Mr. Embry," Mum replied as she stirred her tea. "Go ahead."

"In private, if it please milady."

Mum glanced up at him. "We're all family here," she said. "Whatever you have to say is fine to say in front of Betsy and Gabrielle."

"It's the butcher . . . ," Mr. Embry said.

"What about him?" Mum asked.

"He's—he's here," Mr. Embry choked out. "Demanding payment. He says the bill is—is six weeks past due—"

"*Six* weeks past due?" Mum echoed, but she sounded more amused than upset. "Dear me. No wonder he came to collect! There must be some mistake, Mr. Embry. I always pay the bills on time. If Mr. Crewe did not receive payment, perhaps he forgot to send the bill."

I shifted uncomfortably in my seat, remembering what Juliette had told me about the overdue grocer's bill. It was possible that the butcher had forgotten to send Mum the bill . . . but not the grocer, too.

"Please excuse me," Mum said to Gabrielle and me as she stood up. "I'll write a check to Mr. Crewe right now and return for our tea in a few moments. Mr. Embry, I trust that he presented the bill to you when he arrived?"

"He did, milady," Mr. Embry said.

"Very good. Bring it to the library and we'll settle this matter without delay."

Mum and Mr. Embry left the parlor, leaving me alone with Gabrielle.

"Excuse me," I said, rising abruptly from the table and scurrying after them. I wanted to escape before Gabrielle made more plans for my hair!

In the library, I found Mum poring over her ledger book, with Mr. Embry standing attentively by her side.

"You see?" Mum said, running her finger down a long column of figures. "We did not receive a bill from the butcher in March or April. The oversight was on his part, not ours. And . . ." Mum's voice trailed off as she turned the page. "I don't see bills from the grocer or the milliner, either."

"I beg to differ, milady," Mr. Embry said. "I personally delivered those bills to you a few days ago."

"But, Mr. Embry, I sat down to settle all the accounts just this morning," Mum said with a frown. "The bill folder was empty. If I'd received those bills, I would have paid them. Where did you put them?"

"In the bill folder, as always," replied Mr. Embry.

Mum reached over the ledger. "I'll show you myself, then," she said as she opened the folder. "See? It's empty, just like—"

But the folder wasn't empty. Five, six, seven papers—perhaps more—fluttered to the floor. Even from the doorway, I could see that some had the words PAST DUE stamped on them in red ink.

"This—this can't be," Mum said, her voice shaky, her face pale as moonlight. "I checked the folder *this morning*. It was *empty*—"

"Milady, I give you my word that I placed these bills in the folder days ago," Mr. Embry told her.

"Come away, Betsy," said a low voice in my ear.

It was Gabrielle. I had no idea how long she'd been standing behind me, or how much she had heard. Enough, I supposed, as I stepped into the hall with her.

Enough to know that Mum had failed to pay not just one or two bills, but a whole stack of them.

Enough to know that something at Chatswood Manor was very, very wrong.

7

A few days later, Madame Lorraine arrived after breakfast for an important fitting for Gabrielle's gown. I breathed a sigh of relief as they disappeared into Gabrielle's room, shutting the door behind them; it would be wonderful to spend the next several hours away from Gabrielle's bossy orders.

Maybe Mum and I can finally take our walk through the garden, I thought on my way to the library to see if Mum was free. *Or maybe we can even walk to town together!* A morning spent in town, nibbling sticky buns from the bakery and trying on hats at the millinery shop, was one of our favorite pastimes. Maybe, if we had some time away from Gabrielle and the duties of Chatswood Manor, Mum could tell me her secret.

And maybe I could finally ask her to tell me the truth about Chatswood Manor's finances.

But when I reached the library, Mum wasn't alone. Maggie was standing beside her desk, wearing a somber expression; Mum's back was turned to me, so I couldn't see if she was upset, but her voice sounded very serious indeed. "Thank you for telling me, Maggie," Mum was saying. "And if you should notice—"

It was rude to interrupt, but I didn't want them to think I was eavesdropping again! So I knocked on the door with three quick raps.

"Betsy," Mum said warmly as she turned in her chair. "If you wouldn't mind waiting outside for just a moment while I finish speaking with Maggie—"

Outside? I thought in surprise. *Are they talking about me? Have I done something wrong and Maggie's telling Mum all about it?*

Then I remembered how cross I'd been with Maggie when she interrupted my chat with Juliette. My cheeks started to burn.

"No, milady. I'm quite finished," Maggie said. I noticed that she scarcely looked in my direction, which made me feel even worse. "Thank you for your time."

As soon as we were alone, I braced myself for a

lecture from Mum. Instead, though, she smiled at me and said, "How are you, Betsy?"

"I'm fine, Mum," I replied. "What were you and Maggie discussing?"

Mum's smile faded. "I'm afraid that's got to stay between Maggie and me."

"Another secret?" I cried. "One more thing that I'm not allowed to know?"

"Please calm yourself, Betsy," Mum began.

"Ahem." Mr. Embry cleared his throat discreetly as he stepped into the library. "Pardon the intrusion, Lady Beth, but a telegram from America has just arrived. Per your instructions, I have brought it directly to you."

"At last!" Mum exclaimed as Mr. Embry gave her the telegram. She was beaming as she ripped open the envelope . . . but in a matter of moments, her face filled with despair.

"No!" Mum cried, crumpling the telegram into a ball. "How could this have happened?"

"What?" I asked. "What happened, Mum?"

"I am sorry, Betsy, but I cannot discuss this with you," Mum said shortly. She turned to Mr. Embry. "Have there been other telegrams from America?" she demanded.

"Yes, milady, at least three," Mr. Embry said, surprised. "I have personally delivered them to your desk."

"I didn't receive any of them," Mum said.

"But I placed them on—"

Wham!

I jumped as Mum pounded her fist on the desk—and so did Mr. Embry.

"This is *unacceptable*!" she exclaimed. "How am I to move mountains overseas if I cannot trust my own staff to deliver my bills and telegrams?"

Mr. Embry pulled himself up to his full height. "Milady, I assure you—"

Mum interrupted him. "I am not in need of assurances. I am in need of timely delivery of important papers that require my attention at once. From now on, Mr. Embry, you are to bring any papers that arrive to me *directly* and *immediately*, no matter what else is occupying me when they arrive."

"As you wish, milady," Mr. Embry said stiffly. "If there's nothing else you need from me—"

"No, nothing," Mum replied curtly. "You are dismissed."

Mr. Embry bowed low and left the room without another word.

Mum turned away from me and leaned against the desk with her head bowed.

"Mum, please," I begged. "What's happened? Please, Mum, you've got to tell me. Is it Kay—or Aunt Kate—"

"They're fine, to the best of my knowledge," Mum replied without turning around. "More than that I cannot say."

"But why? Why won't you tell me? You can trust me, Mum. I promise I won't—"

"I heard the shouting," Gabrielle said breathlessly as she rushed into the room, pushing past me on her way to Mum. "What happened, Beth?"

At last Mum turned around, her eyes wet with tears. "Oh, Gabrielle," she began. "I'm too late to—"

Then Mum looked at me sorrowfully. She crossed the room and gave me a hug. "I *am* sorry, Betsy," she said. "But I must ask you to leave us."

She's going to tell Gabrielle, I realized. *But she won't tell me.*

There was nothing for me to do but turn around

and leave the room. I'd barely crossed the threshold when Mum closed the door behind me with a soft *click.*

I stood alone in the hall for a moment, too shocked to move. Whatever secret Mum had been keeping was so big and so bad that she couldn't talk to me—to *me*, her only daughter!—but she would freely share it with Gabrielle. The very thought made me want to cry.

Better move along, I told myself. *I mustn't let Maggie catch me out here. She'll surely tell Mum that I've been eavesdropping again.*

With nowhere else to go, and nothing to do, I returned to my room. Should I unburden myself in a letter to Kay? I still needed to finish my letter to her. But what could I possibly write? *Kay, something terrible is happening, and Mum won't tell me a word about it, but the telegram she just received from America brought her to tears. Do you know what's going on?*

How could I add these worries to my cousin's own burdens?

But what if Kay already knew Mum's secret? It had all started with that phone call from Aunt Kate. . . . If Kay knew, and I could ask her . . .

But I can't ask her, I thought. *I don't even know where she lives.*

It was hopeless.

I glanced out my window at the pale pink blossoms on the cherry trees, fluttering in the warm spring breeze. It would've been such a lovely day to walk to town with Mum. . . .

Then something out the window caught my eye.

It was Mum and Gabrielle, wearing their smart spring coats, walking briskly along the drive.

Walking toward town.

My chest was so tight that I felt like I could hardly breathe. *Mum's off to town with Gabrielle,* I thought numbly. *It never even occurred to her that I might want to go, too. She didn't even bother to tell me that she was leaving.*

As I watched Mum walk away, I felt as though we'd never be able to close the distance growing between us. Tears pricked at my eyes as I thought about how much things had changed between Mum and me ever since Aunt Kate's phone call—and all for the worse. *It's like Mum doesn't trust me anymore,* I thought, wiping the back of my hand across my eyes. *It's like she doesn't even love me.*

There was only one person in Chatswood Manor who could make me feel better, I realized. I could already picture it; Juliette would see how upset I was and tell Eloise to take over for a bit, and then we'd sit somewhere quiet—the pantry, perhaps—and she'd listen to the whole story. And maybe with a friend like Juliette on my side, I'd start to feel better about everything.

I set off for the kitchen at once, but on the way there, something curious happened. I noticed Juliette slipping out of the library.

That's odd, I thought, puzzled. I'd just seen Mum walking toward town, so there was no way that she'd rung for Juliette.

"Juliette!" I called.

She continued on to the kitchen as if she hadn't heard me.

"Juliette!" I said, louder this time.

At last, Juliette stopped. "Lady Betsy," she said. "Can I help you?"

"I was just on my way to see you," I told her. "What were you doing in the library?"

Juliette pursed her lips. "I had hoped to see your mother," she explained in a low voice.

"Is something wrong?"

"Well . . . you see, Lady Betsy . . . it's about your birthday dinner."

"What about it?"

Juliette sighed. "Bernadette brought me a list of dishes that Lady Gabrielle wants served," she continued. "Veal scaloppine. Truffle omelet. And blini with caviar imported all the way from Russia! These special ingredients are *very* expensive, you see, so I thought I'd best make sure that Lady Beth would be willing to purchase them."

A hot wave of anger surged through me. Gabrielle *knew* that the estate was struggling—she was there when all those past-due bills fluttered to the floor—and yet she had ordered Juliette to prepare the most expensive meal she could. And to pass it off as something special for *my* birthday. Why, I didn't even like caviar!

"Where does she find the *nerve*?" I asked Juliette through clenched teeth. "None of that will be necessary. I would like a very simple meal for my birthday dinner, please. Let's see. . . . Would you be able to make . . . new potatoes in cream, buttered peas, and roast chicken? Yes, I think that would be quite nice."

"Lady Betsy, you are a gem," Juliette said. "You are a credit to your mother. If only she realized—truly realized—how lucky she is to have a daughter like you."

My smile went all wobbly; I tried to hide it, but Juliette noticed, of course.

"You think I am just saying that to flatter you, but it's the truth!" she said earnestly. "Look at your poor mother, all these trips to town, begging for a loan, while here at home, you sacrifice again and again—"

"Begging for a loan?" I interrupted. Surely that wasn't what Juliette had said. Surely I had misheard her.

"I am so sorry, Lady Betsy," Juliette said. "I know that your mother has tried to shelter you, but I hate knowing that such a secret is being kept from you. I know you are mature enough to hear the truth, even though it's not my place to tell you. Oh . . . please forget I said anything!"

"Of course I can't forget!" I cried. "Are things really so bad that Mum's been begging? And if things are so dire, why is Mum allowing Gabrielle to run up such bills on things like groceries and fancy gowns?"

Juliette bit her lip and glanced over her shoulder into the empty corridor behind us. "I'm afraid I have heard that it is indeed that bad. But we shouldn't discuss this here," she whispered. "And I need to start the meringues. Come with me."

I followed Juliette to the kitchen. As luck would have it, Eloise and Daphne were polishing silver in the scullery, so it was just the two of us.

"Juliette, it doesn't make any *sense*," I exclaimed. "Mum's been a keen manager of Chatswood Manor for years and years—more than a decade! So why would it all go to pieces now?"

"Overspending, perhaps?" Juliette guessed as she began to break some eggs into a bowl.

I shook my head. "She's very frugal, and practical to a fault. No, there must be something else going on." I tapped my fingers on the butcher block. "What if . . . ? No, it doesn't make sense . . . but *none* of this does. . . ."

"What are you thinking?" asked Juliette.

"What if—promise you won't laugh—what if someone were trying to sabotage Mum?"

Juliette paused; a slimy egg white slid through her fingers. "Sabotage? Why?"

"Well, to make her look incompetent," I said, figuring out my thoughts as I spoke. "You know, someone inside the house could hide the bills and the telegrams from her, that sort of thing. To make it seem like Mum isn't capable of managing Chatswood."

Juliette furiously whisked the bowl full of egg whites. "But who would do such a thing?"

"I haven't figured that part out yet," I admitted. "I suppose it could be anyone who works here, really—"

"Or a visitor."

"Cousin Gabrielle?" I asked in surprise.

"I was going to say your cousin's staff," Juliette said. "But now that you mention it . . . well, it was strange, wasn't it? The way Lady Gabrielle *insisted* on visiting?"

"Yes, it was indeed strange, but I'm still not sure it's her."

"Though I can't imagine what motive her *staff* would have to sabotage your mother."

"But what motive would Gabrielle have?" I replied. "If Gabrielle really is penniless, as the advisers fear, then why would she want to sabotage my mum? Wouldn't it make more sense for her to come here and ask for a loan?"

"What better target than your mother, the heir to the Chatswood fortune?" Juliette said quickly. I noticed she was whipping the egg whites faster and faster. "If she could convince the advisers that your mother was mismanaging the estate and find a way to wrest control of the family fortune, just think of the possibilities! Lady Gabrielle *is* a blood relative, correct?"

"Yes," I replied, as a dreadful sinking feeling settled in the pit of my stomach. "I mean, she's not a descendant of the Chatswood line, but she and Mum shared the same great-grandmother, Cecily."

"I have seen lesser relations weasel their way to more," Juliette said darkly.

"Oh, Juliette," I whispered. "Do you really think that's what's happening?"

But Juliette only shrugged. I could tell she believed it, though. She just didn't want to upset me by saying it.

"What am I going to do?"

"I am sure you'll think of something, milady," Juliette said as she finished whipping the egg whites, which had grown stiff and glossy in the bowl. "A girl as bright as you will figure something out."

I tried to smile, but in truth I felt terrible. Sitting

in the bright, bustling kitchen of Chatswood Manor—the heart of the downstairs—I was suddenly acutely aware that all of it could be slipping away from us, bit by bit, a little more every moment . . . until Mum and I had lost everything.

Just like Cousin Kay and her parents.

I will stop Cousin Gabrielle, I vowed. *No matter what it takes.*

8

At dinner that night, I could barely look at Cousin Gabrielle. Since my conversation with Juliette, I had become even more convinced that my concerns about Gabrielle were well founded. It seemed like the only possible explanation for all the strange occurrences that had plagued us lately—and I was sure it was no coincidence that everything went so wrong right after she arrived.

Juliette must've felt sorry for me after our conversation in the kitchen, for she made one of my favorite meals—lamb medallions and new potatoes—for dinner. But I was so heartsick and angry that I could scarcely eat a bite. Across the table, Gabrielle had no such troubles. My stomach churned with resentment with every bite she took. *That's our silver,* I thought as she brought the fork to her shiny red lips. *That's our food!*

"What you really ought to do is find a husband," Gabrielle lectured Mum after the first course. "It's been ten years since James died, Beth. And you don't want to be rattling around in this big old house all by yourself after Betsy goes to boarding school."

Boarding school? I thought in shock. Chatswood Manor was my *home*. I would never leave it willingly! *What is Gabrielle talking about?*

I looked expectantly at Mum, waiting for her to tell Gabrielle that she would never send me away. But Mum was, as usual these days, preoccupied by something else. "I'm sorry?"

Gabrielle waved her fork in my direction. "Boarding school for Betsy. At the earliest possible opportunity."

"No!" I exclaimed, perhaps a little too loudly—for everyone in the room turned to look at me. "I won't *ever* leave Chatswood Manor. And certainly not for *boarding school*!"

Gabrielle laughed at my outburst. "Betsy, Betsy, *ma chère*, you don't know what you're talking about," she said smoothly. "I went to boarding school when I was fifteen years old, and my only regret is that my parents didn't send me sooner. After all, just look at me now!"

Yes, look at you, I thought angrily. *Destitute and trying to swindle my mum—your own cousin—out of her inheritance!*

"Besides, it's high time you saw the world a bit—and learned to live on your own," Gabrielle continued. "This town is quaint, but far too provincial for a girl of your heritage."

"Is it?" I asked icily. "Then why are you here?"

Gabrielle placed her fork beside her plate. *"Pardonnez-moi?"*

"Betsy," Mum said, a warning in her voice. But I ignored her and plowed ahead.

"If Chatswood Manor is so beneath you, I can't imagine what keeps you here. Please, go; you needn't stay on our account."

"Elizabeth Northrop," Mum said sharply. "That is quite enough."

"But, Mum—"

"Mr. Embry," Mum continued, "please see that the rest of Betsy's dinner is sent to her room."

"As you wish, Lady Beth."

Then Mum turned back to me. "You're excused, Betsy. You'll spend the remainder of the evening in your room considering your disgraceful rudeness. Tomorrow Cousin Gabrielle and I will hear your apology."

I had no choice but to rise from the table with as much dignity as I could muster—but it wasn't easy, considering how my face was burning with shame. On my way out of the room, I could hear Mum begin to apologize to Gabrielle on my behalf.

But I didn't hear her say one word against Gabrielle's suggestion that I be sent away.

In my room, I blinked back hot, angry tears as I sat down at my desk. Writing to Cousin Kay was the *only* thing I could think to do that would make me feel better after the dreadful day I'd had. I wrote and wrote and wrote, not pausing for a moment, not when my hand started to cramp, not even when a tear slipped down my cheek and smudged some of the ink.

At some point, there was a soft knock at the door, but I didn't answer.

The knock came again.

Go away, I thought.

But the door creaked open.

I looked up hopefully. It *had* to be Mum; no one

else in the house would dare enter without my permission. *She's come to hear my side of things,* I thought as a wave of relief washed over me.

But it wasn't Mum. It was Maggie, carrying a tray of sandwiches. I turned back to my letter to hide my disappointment.

"I've brought some supper, milady," she said a quiet voice.

"No, thank you."

"Please, milady; I know your mother is eager for you to complete your meal."

"I'm not hungry."

There was a long silence before Maggie spoke again. "I'll have to tell your mother that you've refused your supper, then."

"I'm sure you were planning to report back to her anyway."

And with that, Maggie finally left me in peace so that I could conclude my letter.

Mum said that I could come out when I'm ready to apologize to Cousin

Gabrielle—but I can't bear it, Kay! I can't! She's the one who owes us an apology! I've got to find a way to make Mum understand what Gabrielle's up to . . . but how? It will be especially hard to prove what Gabrielle is plotting if I'm trapped in my room. Oh, Kay, it seems so hopeless. Perhaps I'll have to apologize after all. But only if I absolutely have no other choice. What I've got to do is find a way to prove to Mum that Gabrielle is scheming to take her fortune. The only question is . . . how?

When morning came, Maggie's knock at my door was earlier than expected. "Good morning, milady," she said, as if the unpleasantness of the night before was a distant memory. "I've brought you a boiled egg and some toast—and a nice pot of tea. I thought you might be a bit peckish."

I hated to admit it, but I was ravenous. Sending away my supper had seemed like a good idea at the time, but I had come to regret it as the hours passed.

"Thank you, Maggie," I said stiffly. To be honest, I was a bit embarrassed by her kindness.

We didn't speak much as Maggie helped me dress for the day. "How would you like to wear your hair, milady?" she asked.

"Oh, I don't care." I sighed. As long as apologizing to Gabrielle hung over my head, I knew I'd be able to think of little else. *Better get it over with,* I told myself. *Besides, you've got more important things to worry about.* "Listen, Maggie, when you're done, if you wouldn't mind telling Mum—"

"I surely will, milady, but she's just left for town," Maggie replied.

"For town?" I repeated.

"Yes. I heard her telling Mr. Embry last night that she had an early appointment," Maggie continued. "But as soon as she's back, I'll be certain to tell her that you'd like to see her."

"Yes, Maggie, please do," I said. A plan was unfurling in my mind—a foolhardy one, to be certain, but the more I considered it, the more convinced I became that it just might work. "And, you know, I think I'll just wear my hair down today. There's no need for you to fuss with it. I can brush it myself."

"Very well, milady," Maggie said. "Is there anything else you need?"

"No, Maggie. Thank you."

Somehow I made myself sit quietly while I waited for Maggie to finish in my room. *Stay calm,* I told myself as I took a bite of toast. *Act normally.*

The instant Maggie was gone, I dropped my scone on the plate and rushed to the wardrobe. I pulled on my shoes and grabbed my cream-colored coat. And then—expressly disobeying my mother—I left my room.

I couldn't believe how easy it was to walk out of Chatswood Manor all on my own. Surely every footman and housemaid had heard about the scene at dinner—and my embarrassing punishment—but not a single one dared to stop me. The feeling of freedom was positively dizzying! There was a cheerful spring in my step as I set off down the twisty path that led to the heart of town. I couldn't believe that this plan hadn't occurred to me sooner. *Of course* a trip to town could help me find the evidence I needed to prove to Mum what Gabrielle had been plotting. Perhaps I could ask around a bit to learn who, exactly, had been spreading rumors about Mum's finances. If the description matched my cousin, I'd have proof—and a witness. Mum would *have* to believe me then, no matter how fond she was of Gabrielle. And if I walked quickly enough, I might even be able to find out the purpose of Mum's appointment. Was she really attempting to get a loan . . . or was there another reason for all her trips to town recently? *Just because Mum's keeping a whole pack of secrets from me doesn't mean I can't find them out,* I thought with determination.

I could already imagine how it would go when I told Mum about Gabrielle's schemes. . . . She would be shocked at first, but then she'd be so grateful to me for uncovering them and saving Chatswood Manor! Of course, Gabrielle would be sent away at once. *Then all the unpleasantness of the last few weeks will disappear,* I thought, fairly skipping as I came to a bend in the road, *and things between Mum and me will be just as wonderful as they've always—*

"Betsy!"

It was my mother, sitting on a stone bench just off the path, looking positively astonished to see me. I stopped dead in my tracks and stared at her.

Mum stood up right away. "What are—how did—why—"

"I—I—"

"Who said you could leave Chatswood Manor? Or your room, for that matter?" Mum continued. "Are you going to town? *Alone?*"

"I—"

"Are you *following* me?"

"I—"

"Answer my questions!"

"I would if you'd give me a chance!"

I'm not sure who was more surprised that I'd raised my voice—Mum or me. I'd never yelled at her before, not once in all my life.

Mum looked at me for a long moment. "Fair enough. Go ahead, Betsy. I'm listening."

I took a deep breath. This was it—my chance to make things right.

"I did leave the house—and my room—without

permission," I began. "I know more about what's going on than you've told me. I think—I think I know more about it than you do."

"Is that so?" Mum asked evenly. "Go on."

"I know that there've been troubles with the accounts and that people think that we've nearly exhausted the inheritance."

"I told you to not to worry about that."

"But how could I *not* worry about it, Mum?" I asked. "Aunt Kate wasn't worried, and look what happened to her. If we're on the brink of losing everything—just like our American relatives—"

A pained expression crossed Mum's face. "Oh, Betsy," she murmured. "This has been weighing so heavily on you, hasn't it?"

"*All* the secrets have!" I exclaimed as my eyes welled with tears. "I don't want to lose Chatswood Manor, Mum! It's our *home*! Where would we go? How would we live? What would happen to us?"

Mum immediately wrapped her arms around me. "Chatswood Manor is on sound financial footing, and you needn't take my word on it," she said. "We'll go to the bank. We'll go right now and have a chat with

Mr. Mageary. If you see the accounts with your own eyes, my darling, you'll know that there is nothing to worry about. I've taken many precautions to protect the inheritance during these years of financial uncertainty, and I'm pleased to say that we've weathered the storm."

"Then why have you been keeping so many secrets from me?" I asked. "We've never had secrets before, but now you won't tell me anything. Don't you trust me anymore? Why—"

I swallowed hard as a lump filled my throat. And then, to my surprise, I saw Mum blink back tears as well.

"Come, Betsy. Sit with me," Mum said as she led me over to the stone bench. When we were both seated, she took my hands in hers. "First, I owe you an apology. You're right; I shouldn't have kept so many secrets from you. It's a mother's job to protect her child, but you're not much of a child anymore, are you? And I see quite clearly that in trying to shield you from a painful truth, I've only caused you greater heartache. For that, dear Betsy, I am sorry. Please know that the trust I place in you has never wavered. Not once."

I tried to smile, but the words "painful truth" hung heavily in the air between us.

"And so let me make things right by telling you now," Mum continued. "You remember, of course, the phone call I received from Aunt Kate a few weeks ago?"

"Yes."

"You're right that there was something she told me in that call that I've kept from you."

I could tell from her voice that it was bad news. "Is it about Cousin Kay?" I cried, my heart pounding.

Mum shook her head. "No . . . well, not exactly," she replied. "You see, darling, Uncle Joseph—well, we must try with all our might not to judge him for what he has done. Remember, Betsy, that he committed this act with the best of intentions—to protect Aunt Kate and Kay from destitution. And when you look at it like that, you can see that there is a certain sort of . . . nobility to it."

"Oh, Mum," I whispered. "What did he do?"

"He took the Katherine necklace from Aunt Kate's dressing table . . . and he sold it."

I gasped in horror. "He *sold* it? He *sold* the Katherine necklace?"

"Yes. But—"

"He had no right! It doesn't belong to him—he had *no right*!"

"No, Betsy, he didn't," Mum said. "Aunt Kate was livid."

I leaped off the bench and began pacing back and forth. "We've got to buy it back," I said urgently. "Mum, can't we wire the money and—"

"Betsy, darling, I know this news comes as a shock, but please let me finish before you upset yourself further," Mum said, pulling me back to the bench. I sat down with reluctance. It was hard to keep still when all I wanted was to run the rest of the way to town, withdraw the money from our accounts, and wire it to America immediately!

"When Aunt Kate and I spoke on the phone, she had just discovered what Uncle Joseph had done," Mum continued. "You can imagine how upset she was. Of course I offered to buy back the necklace immediately, but Aunt Kate didn't yet know which pawnshop held it, or how much the price would be. So we agreed that she would send me the information by telegram as soon as possible so that I could wire the money directly to the shop at once.

"The only problem is that the telegram never came—and, as you remember, Aunt Kate no longer had a phone or even a reliable address that I could use to reach them. And when I finally did receive a telegram from Aunt Kate, it contained the worst possible news: Somehow, her first and second telegrams never reached me, and during that delay, the pawnshop sold the necklace to someone else."

"So it's gone, then?" I asked numbly. "The Katherine necklace is really and truly gone?"

To my surprise, Mum smiled. "No, Betsy, and that's the wonderful news. I've found the man who bought it, and as luck would have it, he's just arrived in London on business!"

"Really?" I cried.

Mum nodded happily. "Yes, really. And best of all, he's agreed to sell the Katherine necklace to me. In fact, I'm on my way to town to send him a telegram to confirm that I will meet him at the Savoy in London in two days' time! Then we'll have the Katherine necklace safe and sound until we can return it to Aunt Kate and Kay. Not via the post, though. . . . Once the necklace is in my possession, I shan't part with it until I put it directly in Kate's hands."

"Post?" I asked. "You mean you've got their new address?"

"Why, yes, Betsy, didn't I tell you?" Mum asked in surprise. "Aunt Kate included it in her telegram. The news about the Katherine necklace was so heartbreaking that it must've slipped my mind to tell you."

"That's all right," I told her. "I've been writing a letter to Kay ever since the phone call."

"Oh, I feel just dreadful," Mum replied. "I'm sorry, Betsy. You'll be able to mail your letter today."

"Where are they living now?"

"For the foreseeable future, they'll remain at Vandermeer Manor in the groundskeeper's cottage," Mum explained.

"So they haven't lost their home?"

"No. Not yet."

I put my hand to my head, feeling almost dizzy with gratitude for this unexpectedly happy ending. It had been such a whirlwind of news that I felt quite overwhelmed.

"Betsy," Mum said suddenly. "Would you like to

come to London with me to purchase the Katherine necklace?"

"Oh, would I!" I exclaimed as I hugged Mum. "Thank you, Mum!"

"We'll make a day of it, just the two of us," Mum promised. "Shopping in the morning, lunch at the Savoy, perhaps a visit to the Victoria and Albert Museum in the afternoon. An early birthday present!"

A perfect birthday present, I thought as I rested my head against Mum's shoulder. "I hated having secrets between us."

"As did I," Mum replied. "But sometimes secrets are necessary—vital, even—whether we like them or not."

I squirmed a bit on the hard stone bench. I still hadn't told Mum my theory that Gabrielle was behind all the mean-spirited gossip—but this didn't seem like the right time, especially since I didn't have proof. I didn't want to do anything that might upset Mum, or harm our relationship just when we'd finally mended it.

I'll keep quiet about my suspicions for now, I decided. *The time to tell Mum is when I have proof—and not before.*

"Let's continue on to town," Mum said. "After we

telegram the American gentleman—his name is Mr. O'Brien—we'll pop by the bakery. I don't know about you, but I think a sticky bun would be quite nice."

I grinned at Mum. Of course she knew that sticky buns were my favorite. But what I'd enjoy the most would be sharing one with her.

9

I'd thought that nothing could top the perfectly lovely morning Mum and I spent in town—but there was even better news awaiting us when we got home. The moment we returned, Mr. Embry approached us, carrying a silver tray with a pale yellow envelope and a letter opener.

"A letter from Lady Gabrielle," he explained as he presented the tray to Mum.

"A letter?" Mum asked. She read it right there in the entryway. "How peculiar," Mum said when she finished. "Cousin Gabrielle has been unexpectedly called away on an errand. She hopes to be back in time for your birthday, Betsy, and says that she wants to be there when you receive the Elizabeth necklace."

"An errand?" I echoed. "What sort of errand?"

"She doesn't say," replied Mum. "It's quite mysterious, really."

More like suspicious, I thought. But then I decided to enjoy the break from Gabrielle as long as it lasted. Besides, maybe some time away from Gabrielle would help Mum see her for who she really was.

"Betsy, if you'll excuse me, I have some business to attend to," Mum said. "Make sure you tell Maggie about our trip to London. She'll want to make sure your traveling clothes are in order."

"I will, Mum. And thank you again. Thank you for everything!" I told her.

Instead of ringing for Maggie, though, I went downstairs to find her—mainly because I also wanted to pop by the kitchen to see Juliette. I knew she'd be just as pleased as I was to learn that Gabrielle was gone . . . for a few days, at least.

As soon as she saw me, Juliette stopped what she was doing and hurried over.

"I heard all about last night," she said in a breathless whisper. "Horrid. Just dreadful, really, that that miserable woman enjoys a meal at *your* table while you're banished to your room. You poor, poor dear."

"Oh, that?" I said with a shrug. "That's no matter.

It's over and done with, anyway. Besides, I have good news—Gabrielle is gone!"

Juliette's eyes grew wide with surprise. "*Gone?* Just like that?" she exclaimed. "How can this be? No one has said a word—"

"It just happened," I explained. "She left a note for Mum—something about an errand that would take her away for a few days. Hopefully, she won't come back!"

"Well, that *is* good news," replied Juliette. "No wonder you look so cheerful, milady."

"That's not all," I said. "In two days, Mum's taking me to London!"

"Really!" Juliette said. "What a surprise. I'm sure you and your mother will have a delightful time . . . though everything in London *is* very expensive. Did your mother give a reason for the visit? Perhaps she has an appointment at one of the banks? Oh, do you think she is asking for a loan?"

I shook my head vehemently. "Oh, no, nothing like that. We're going because . . ." My voice trailed off as I wondered if I should tell Juliette about the Katherine necklace. Mum hadn't said it was a secret . . . but it felt like it should be one. "I'm sorry, but I really can't say."

"You *can't* say?" Juliette repeated. "Or you *won't* say?"

I smiled apologetically, my lips sealed.

Juliette abruptly turned away from me, smoothing her apron as she approached the counter. "You're not the only one with a secret. I have one of my own."

My curiosity immediately got the better of me. "What is it?"

"I don't dare tell . . . not unless you promise that you won't tell another living soul."

"I promise."

For a long moment, she was silent, and I wondered if Juliette had thought better of sharing her secret. Then, at last, she spoke.

"I have a sister. Her name is Helena," she began.

"I didn't know that you have a sister!" I exclaimed. It seemed odd that during all our conversations, Juliette had never once mentioned her.

"She started out in service, just like me," continued Juliette. "She was a lady's maid to a prominent French family with a dreadfully spoiled daughter. Helena did her best to please the miserable girl, but there was nothing my sister could do that would satisfy her.

Then, one terrible day, Helena was blamed for something the horrible daughter had *ordered* her to do. She lost her position and was dismissed without a reference. It brought shame to my entire family."

"I'm so sorry, Juliette," I said. "That's dreadful."

"That's not even the worst of it," Juliette said. "Without a reference, Helena was never able to find another position in service. Her entire life depends on the charity of others. Without our family, my sister would be a pauper."

"There's nothing more important than family," I agreed. "Helena is lucky to have a sister like you."

Juliette looked as if she wanted to say something else, but she held her tongue.

"You know, you should tell Mum about Helena," I suggested. "I don't think there are any positions open right now, but perhaps Mum would hire Helena as a housemaid. Or a scullery maid! Then you two could work together in the kitchen."

"Non, non, non!" Juliette said rapidly. "*Non,* milady. This is why I swore you to secrecy, and why I never speak of my sister. I was forced to leave France to escape the cloud of suspicion that hung over our family. If the

others at Chatswood learned of the accusations against Helena . . . what would they think of me? What if I too lost my position in disgrace?"

"That will never happen," I assured Juliette. "You mustn't worry about such things, Juliette. Your secret is safe with me."

"Thank you, milady," she replied. "So why is your mother taking you to London?"

I shook my head. "I already told you it's a secret."

"But I told you *my* secret," Juliette pressed. "So now you must tell me yours."

"I'm very sorry, but I can't," I said. "I can't tell anyone, not even Cousin Kay. Which reminds me, I've got to finish the letter I've been writing to her so that I can send it off with the afternoon post. Can you believe that—"

But Juliette had turned her back on me. "I'm very busy at the moment, Lady Betsy. My apologies that I can't entertain you any longer today."

I'm sure Juliette meant no harm, but her abrupt dismissal felt like a slap. "Of course," I said when I recovered my composure. "I'm sorry that I interrupted you."

Then I left the kitchen straightaway. But before I returned to my room, I remembered that the whole point of going downstairs was to tell Maggie about my upcoming trip to London. I found her in the servants' common room, attending to a bit of darning.

"Of course, milady. I'll see to your traveling suit today," Maggie told me. "A light steam and an airing outside will do the trick."

"Thank you very much," I told her. "Now, if you'll excuse me, I have a letter to send—at last!"

On the way back to my room, I stopped by the library to get a stamp from Mum, and we chatted for a bit about which hat would look best with my traveling suit. Then I really had to scurry to get my letter ready for the afternoon post! My desk was so untidy that it took me a moment to find an envelope, and as soon as I did, I addressed it to Cousin Kay, then reached for the letter I'd been writing to her for the last few weeks.

There was just one problem: It wasn't in the drawer where I'd left it.

I shuffled through the papers on the top of my desk, but the letter wasn't there, either.

After an hour spent searching my entire bedroom

and asking Maggie and the housemaids if they'd seen my letter, there was only one conclusion to be reached.

My letter to Cousin Kay—all eight pages of it—had disappeared.

10

Two days later, Mum and I took the early train to London. I was so excited about the trip that I didn't even mind waking up before dawn! The sun was well up by the time we arrived, bathing the bustling city in beautiful golden light. Compared to the stillness of the countryside around Chatswood Manor, the noisy bustle of London made it seem like the kind of place where *anything* could happen.

Mum and I spent the morning shopping, just as she'd promised. Though we saw many fine things, from stylish hats and elegant shoes to lavish parasols and decadent jewelry, it was hard to concentrate on them, knowing that the Katherine necklace awaited us at the Savoy.

"There's just one more stop before we meet with Mr. O'Brien," Mum told me as she paused before a blue sign that read BILLINGHAM'S STATIONERY AND PAPER GOODS. "Here we are."

"What's this?" I asked as we entered the store.

"I've been thinking about your writing," Mum replied. "The women in our family have always had a knack for writing, going back to Elizabeth Chatswood herself. But it's different for you, Betsy. I think you have a real talent for it."

I smiled, delighted by Mum's praise.

"I've been very moved by your determination to correspond with Cousin Kay," continued Mum. "And so I've decided that we must outfit you with everything you need to continue on this path. What do you say, Betsy? Would you like to have your very own typewriter?"

"A typewriter?" I cried. "Of my very own?"

Mum nodded, pleased, as the clerk approached us. "We'd like to see a British Oliver, I think, and we'll need extra ribbons for it, of course," she said.

"Certainly, madam," he replied.

The British Oliver typewriter was a gorgeous machine, glossy black all over with gold trim and smooth, cream-colored keys. The clerk showed me how to insert a crisp sheet of paper and how to change the ribbon. Then he said that I could give it a try!

I rested my hands lightly on the keys, just the way he showed me, as I pondered what my very first typewritten words should be.

`My name is Elizabeth Northrop.`

`Tomorrow is my twelfth birthday.`

The *clackety-clack* of the keys leaping up to strike the ribbon was louder than I expected. Just like magic, my words appeared on the blank page, as neat as a pin.

"Mum, I absolutely adore it!" I cried. "Thank you so much!"

"You're very welcome, my darling," she replied with an indulgent smile. "I can't wait to read what you'll write with it."

When the purchase was complete, Mum made arrangements for the parcels to be held for us at the train station. Then we set off for the Savoy. My heart was beating so hard that I could hear it pounding in my ears. In moments, I would see the Katherine necklace with my very own eyes! What would it feel like to hold it in my hands? I'd already decided that I wouldn't try it on—not even once. No, the very next person to wear it would be my cousin Kay. It was only right.

We arrived at the Savoy promptly at half-past twelve and waited for Mr. O'Brien in the lobby. Every time the lift doors opened, I jumped; but after twenty long minutes, we were still waiting.

"Since Mr. O'Brien is a guest at the hotel, we'd better telephone his room to see how much longer he expects to be delayed," Mum finally said. "I must say, I'm surprised that he didn't send word to us if he was going to be late."

I followed Mum to the front desk, where one of the clerks dialed Mr. O'Brien's room for her. After he answered the phone, the clerk passed it to Mum.

"Hello, Mr. O'Brien. This is Lady Etheridge-Northrop," she said. "My daughter, Betsy, and I are here to conduct the transaction we discussed and were wondering when you might be available to join us."

There was a pause while Mum listened. "Yes, we're here," she repeated, a quizzical expression on her face.

"Right downstairs. Yes. I see. Very good."

Then she returned the phone to the clerk.

"Mum, what did he say?" I asked. "Is he on his way?"

"He seemed surprised to hear from me," Mum said. "I can't imagine that he forgot our meeting. Perhaps he's so preoccupied with his business dealings that our appointment slipped his mind."

"Perhaps," I said.

A few moments later, a tall man walked out of the lift. I noticed right away that he was very dashing, with jet-black hair and a smart gray suit. The moment he saw us, he seemed to know who we were, and he crossed the lobby with long, confident strides.

"You must be Lady Etheridge-Northrop," he said to Mum in an American accent. "I'm Patrick O'Brien. And is this Lady Betsy?"

"We're very pleased to make your acquaintance," Mum said.

"Would you join me in the parlor?" he replied. "It's right this way."

That's when I noticed that Mr. O'Brien was empty-handed. *Where is the Katherine necklace?* I wondered. *Is it in the hotel safe?*

Mum and I sat together on a love seat across from Mr. O'Brien, who crossed and uncrossed his legs as if he couldn't get comfortable in his chair. Then he leaned forward, leaned back, and finally, clasping his hands, said, "I can't think of a way to tell you this, so I should probably just come out with it. I think there's been a terrible misunderstanding."

No, I thought. *Oh, no.* My hand reached for Mum, who stayed remarkably calm—on the outside, at least—as she asked, "Where is the Katherine necklace, Mr. O'Brien?"

Mr. O'Brien leaned forward again. "It's been sold to another party, and I can't begin to tell you how sorry I am."

Sold! I thought in horror. Mum squeezed my hand so hard that her knuckles turned white.

"I should like to know how that happened," Mum replied in a steely voice. "We had an agreement—"

"I'd also like to know," he said fervently. "Two days ago, I received your telegram confirming our meeting for today. But later that afternoon, I received a second telegram from you proposing that we meet the previous day—which was yesterday."

"I sent no such telegram."

"I can see that," Mr. O'Brien said, removing a silk pocket square from his jacket and wiping his brow. "But the damage was done, I'm afraid. Yesterday, I met with a woman who claimed to be you, and I sold her the necklace. I had no idea that I wasn't dealing with your ladyship."

For a long moment, no one spoke.

"I could just kick myself!" Mr. O'Brien suddenly exclaimed. "Lady Etheridge-Northrop, I truly hope that you can accept my apology. It was my every wish to return the Katherine necklace to you personally. If I'd had *any* idea—"

"Mr. O'Brien, there was no way for you to know that you were dealing with an impostor," Mum said, rising abruptly. "I do appreciate your efforts to resolve this matter, though I'm very sorry that we're unable to come to a more satisfactory conclusion."

"If there's *anything* I can do . . . ," Mr. O'Brien said as he, too, stood up. It was almost as if he knew how much the Katherine necklace meant to my family.

"I do appreciate that," Mum replied with sincerity.

"Good day, Mr. O'Brien, and I wish you safe travels back to America."

"Good-bye," I said softly as Mum and I turned to leave.

I rubbed the back of my neck, which was all prickly with a feeling of something left undone. "Mr. O'Brien," I said suddenly, letting go of Mum's arm as I spun around to face him. "Wait."

"Yes, Lady Betsy?" he asked, raising an eyebrow.

"Could you describe her?"

"Well, she seemed rather . . . glamorous," he began. "She had a hat with one of those large brims, you know, angled over her face. . . ." He gestured vaguely toward his head. "And she wore very dark glasses, like Marlene Dietrich."

I tried to shrug off my disappointment. It made sense that the impostor had gone out of her way to conceal her appearance.

"She did have a rather unusual accent," Mr. O'Brien continued. "Even yesterday, I thought, 'If I didn't know better, I'd guess that Lady Etheridge-Northrop spent some years in France.' If only I'd spoken up—said something—"

France! I thought wildly. *What are the odds that a mysterious French woman stole the Katherine necklace right out from under us—right after Cousin Gabrielle left Chatswood Manor so unexpectedly? Oh, it's just got to be her!*

There was not a shred of doubt in my mind that the stranger who had vanished with the Katherine necklace was none other than Cousin Gabrielle.

11

Mum and I didn't want to go to the Victoria and Albert Museum after everything that had happened, so she rang Chatswood Manor to tell Mr. Embry that we were on our way home. After that, Mum didn't say much of anything, staring silently out the window of the train as we traveled back to Chatswood Manor. I had to find a way to tell her my suspicions about Gabrielle . . . but how? *When Mum realizes that Cousin Gabrielle has the necklace, she'll be crushed,* I thought. I had to choose my words carefully.

I reached out and gingerly tapped her arm, which startled Mum. She looked at me for half an instant as if she'd forgotten that I was there. Then, with a sigh, she wrapped her arm around my shoulders.

"Mum," I began. "Is the Katherine necklace really and truly gone forever? Isn't there *something* we could do? Like—like—hire a private investigator or a detective or a—"

"I suppose so," Mum said in a distracted sort of way.

A flame of hope flickered inside me. "That's splendid! When we get home, we must telephone Mr. O'Brien. I'm sure the detective will want to interview him personally, so Mr. O'Brien mustn't return to America before—"

"This isn't a radio play, darling," Mum said. "Some mysteries are not destined to be solved."

"But—"

"Of course, I will make inquiries about the Katherine necklace," Mum said. "But I should hate for you to get your hopes up. That would only make the disappointment more difficult to bear."

"I won't give up," I told Mum, and I meant every word. "Even if it takes me the rest of my life to find the Katherine necklace."

Mum smiled wistfully at me. "If anyone could find it, I do believe it would be you, Betsy."

"We should—we should make a plan," I pushed on. "Who knew that the Katherine necklace had been sold to Mr. O'Brien? Who even knew that Uncle Joseph had pawned it?"

"That's an excellent point, Betsy," Mum replied thoughtfully. "Someone in England must've known that it was for sale to broker a deal with Mr. O'Brien during his visit."

"Did"—my heart was pounding so hard that I was certain Mum could hear it—"did Cousin Gabrielle know about it?"

Mum fixed me with an intent look. "Yes," she admitted after a pause. "Yes, I confided in Gabrielle when I was waiting for a telegram from Kate. Before I realized that someone was stealing them."

Gabrielle knew! I thought. *She knew all about it!*

"The telegrams that started disappearing right after Gabrielle's arrival?" I asked. "Her letter never said where she was going, did it?"

Mum pursed her lips. I could tell that she understood what I was trying to say.

"No. It can't be Gabrielle. Why would she do such a thing?" Mum said.

"Perhaps she's always wanted one of the Chatswood necklaces for her very own," I told Mum. "After all, she was so jealous of your necklace all those years ago. Perhaps she was just waiting until the opportunity presented itself."

"Though our history is long and complicated," Mum began, "Gabrielle and I have always been bonded by blood. But perhaps she has been playing me false for all these years. . . ."

Mum didn't finish her sentence. She didn't need to. Suddenly, I realized that such a betrayal from Gabrielle would make the loss of the Katherine necklace even worse for Mum. I wasn't particularly fond of Gabrielle, but Mum clearly loved her. I wished more than anything that I could've shielded Mum from this terrible truth.

"It hasn't been easy, you know," Mum said, staring out the window as the train whisked us closer and closer to Chatswood. "Your father and I were supposed to be partners in all of this—managing the estate, raising you. How different it all would've been if he'd been by my side. I've tried so hard, Betsy, to trust my judgment. To make the right decisions—not just for myself and for Chatswood Manor, but for you most of all. I miss your father for so many reasons, but at least at the end of each day, I knew I'd done my best. And my best has always seemed to be good enough. But now . . ."

"Mum!" I exclaimed. "Don't talk like that."

"The Katherine necklace was within my reach," Mum said, almost to herself. "And yet I've let it slip through my fingers, all because of my own carelessness."

"It's *not* your fault that Gabrielle stole the necklace away from us," I said firmly. "And you've done a wonderful job with—with everything. No one could've done better. No one!"

Mum tried to smile at me.

But I could tell that she didn't agree.

When we reached Chatswood Manor, Mr. Embry, Nellie, and Maggie were waiting for us in the great hall.

"Good afternoon, Lady Beth and Lady Betsy," Mr. Embry said. "Welcome back."

"Thank you, Mr. Embry," Mum replied. "Has Lady Gabrielle returned?"

"No, milady," he replied. "Nor has she telephoned."

Mum's shoulders slumped at the news. I wasn't sure how much Nellie knew about the missing Katherine necklace, but she could tell that something was wrong. She stepped forward and reached for Mum's valise as she said, "Welcome back, milady. I'm sure you're tired from your journey. I've drawn a hot bath for you, if you'd like, and I'd be happy to bring some refreshments to your room."

"Thank you, Nellie," Mum said gratefully. "That sounds wonderful. Mr. Embry, are there any messages?"

"Lord Turley telephoned this morning about a matter of some urgency and has requested that you return his call at your earliest convenience. Lady Dandridge stopped by to secure your support for the charity drive, and you've been nominated as head judge for the flower show. There are some staffing matters to attend to as well, and I believe Maggie would appreciate a private audience with you."

I snuck a glance at Maggie, wondering what she wanted to say to Mum in private. *What did I do wrong now?* I wondered. I hadn't even been home all day!

"Finally," Mr. Embry concluded, "I locked the day's post in your desk."

Mum grimaced at all the work awaiting her. "Never mind about that bath, Nellie," she said. "I'll be in the library if anyone needs me."

Then Mum turned to me and kissed my forehead. "I'm sorry that our grand outing turned into such a disappointing misadventure, darling," she said. "But there's no one else in the world I would've rather had by my side today. Thank you for coming with me."

"I'm sorry, too," I replied. "But I was glad to be with you."

I stood in the foyer and watched Mum walk away. Even as tired as she was, the business of Chatswood Manor wouldn't wait. I wished there was something—anything—I could do to help.

At dinner that night, Mum seemed even more subdued than she had been on the train. More than once, I caught her staring into space, and she scarcely touched her food. I couldn't imagine why—I thought Juliette had truly outdone herself by preparing salmon mousse, one of Mum's favorite dishes. But even the small bites Mum forced herself to eat left a look of displeasure on her face.

After dinner, I thought about going downstairs to see Juliette, but I knew she'd have lots of questions about my day in London, and I didn't want to answer any of them. Instead, I went to my room and rang for Maggie to help me get ready for bed. Then I sat at my new typewriter for the very first time. Alone at last, all the emotions I'd tried to quash all day—the shock and outrage and deep disappointment—surged within me. I had to write; it was the only thing I could do. But I couldn't start a new letter to my cousin—not yet. Kay would need to hear the news about the Katherine necklace from her mother.

I placed my fingers on the smooth, cold keys. As I started to type, the keys went *clack-a-clack-a-clack*, slowly at first as I searched for each letter and then a bit faster as I became more familiar with their odd placement.

SCENE: A posh hotel. A MOTHER and DAUGHTER sit on a settee.

PROP MAN: A door SLAMS. We hear FOOTSTEPS.

GENTLEMAN: Allow me to introduce myself. I am the American gentleman, Patrick O'Brien. And I have something for you.

PROP MAN: The soft OPENING of a velvet case.

MOTHER and DAUGHTER gasp.

DAUGHTER: The Katherine necklace! Oh, Mum, it is as beautiful as I imagined.

I paused, frowning at the paper as I pulled it from the typewriter. It certainly looked like a page from a real radio drama, but there was something wholly dissatisfying about it.

Then I felt a gentle hand on my shoulder. I jumped in my seat.

"Mum!"

"I'm sorry, Betsy. I didn't mean to frighten you."

My face turned red as I realized that Mum might've read what I'd written. I crumpled the paper into a ball.

"Betsy! No!" Mum cried.

"It was stupid, just rubbish," I mumbled in embarrassment.

"It was an excellent start," Mum said firmly as she smoothed out the paper.

"But it wasn't . . . *honest*," I replied, trying to express why I was so unhappy with what I'd written. "It was make-believe. Very foolish."

"It is what should've happened today," Mum told me. "And there's nothing foolish about longing for a different outcome. I feel very much the same way, you know. Does it help?"

"Does what help?"

"Writing the alternative. Using your talents to explore what could've—should've—happened."

I thought for a moment before I answered. "Yes, I suppose it does," I admitted.

"Then you must keep at it," Mum said. "The world will be full of people who want to silence you and put you in your place. You must never let yourself become one of them. Promise?"

"Promise," I replied.

"That's a good girl," Mum said. "And now it's bedtime. After all, tomorrow is a *very* special day. You'll want to be well rested for whatever surprises your birthday may hold."

My birthday! Just the thought of my twelfth birthday arriving at last—in a few hours!—made me smile, even after everything that had happened today. How would I ever fall asleep tonight?

After I climbed between the sheets, Mum pulled

the blankets over me and tucked in the sides, just like she used to do when I was small. Then she brushed my hair away from my face and kissed my forehead. Were her eyes especially shiny, or was it just my imagination?

"Mum, stay," I said impulsively. "Tell me stories from when you were a girl . . . stories about Granny and Aunt Kate and your trip to America and *your* twelfth birthday."

She hesitated for a moment. "My darling, nothing would please me more," Mum finally said as she patted my hand, "but I'm afraid that I have some pressing business to attend to. And it simply cannot wait. Good night, my love. I hope your final hours as an eleven-year-old are filled with the sweetest dreams."

And then Mum turned off the light and slipped out of the room, leaving me alone in the dark.

At some point in the night, I must've fallen asleep, because the next thing I knew I awoke with a start. *Today is my birthday!* I thought. *It's* finally *here!*

I threw off the covers and ran across the room to ring for Maggie. I didn't want to waste a moment of my special day by lounging about in bed! But before

I could reach the bellpull, there came a soft knock at the door. I must've slept later than I thought if Maggie had already come to help me get dressed.

"Come in," I called, and as soon as I spoke, the door opened. But it wasn't Maggie after all.

It was Mum, carrying a tray with scones and tea, a saucer of jam, and a single rose in a bud vase.

"Happy birthday, dear Betsy!" Mum exclaimed, beaming as she entered the room.

"Thank you, Mum!" I said. "What are you—"

"I wanted to be the very first to wish you a happy birthday," she replied.

"Is that strawberry jam?" I asked eagerly as I moved toward Mum. "You know that's my favorite. . . ."

My voice trailed off as I got a better look at the tray. For nestled between the vase and the teapot was something entirely unexpected.

A blue velvet jewel box.

My heart fluttered in my chest as I stood there, blinking in surprise and utterly lost for words. Of course I knew that at some point today I would receive the Elizabeth necklace.

But I had never expected it like this.

Mum set the tray down on the dressing table, picked up the box, and led me over to the window seat.

"Usually, the Elizabeth necklace is presented with great ceremony, in front of an audience," Mum said, holding my hands in hers. "In fact, your granny received it at her birthday ball in front of hundreds of people. But so much is different this year. When you came to me a few weeks ago, so determined to cancel your ball, you opened my eyes, Betsy—as you have ever since that day twelve years ago when you entered the world.

"Tradition is important. But not more important than family. And so when I tried to decide the best time to give the necklace to you, I realized that the best time would be when you and I could be together, alone and undisturbed."

Mum deftly opened the jewel box to reveal the Elizabeth necklace in all its glory, gold gleaming, sapphires sparkling in the morning sun. My breath caught in my throat. How could such a lovely thing belong to me?

"Would you like to wear it?"

Mum's voice brought me back from my thoughts. Unable to speak, I simply nodded. In an instant, she draped the Elizabeth necklace around my neck. Its cool weight was something I'd been waiting to feel for my entire life.

"The real meaning of the Elizabeth necklace is not in its precious metal or priceless jewels," Mum continued, "but in the legacy of those who've worn it over the years, passing it down from mother to daughter, Elizabeth to Eliza to Liz to me, and now, my darling, to you. I hope that when you wear the Elizabeth necklace, you will find, as I did, that it connects you to all of them. I think that's what Elizabeth and Katherine hoped would happen when they began this sacred tradition so long ago, giving their necklaces to their own daughters."

At the mention of Katherine, two tears spilled from Mum's eyes, but she didn't wipe them away until the Elizabeth necklace was securely fastened around my neck. It hurt my heart, too, to think of Cousin Kay's upcoming birthday. How wrong it was that Aunt Kate wouldn't be able to give the Katherine necklace to my cousin—wrong in every way.

"Don't cry, Mum," I said. "I know in my heart that the Katherine necklace will end up precisely where it belongs."

Slam!

As the door to my bedroom banged open, Mum and I both jumped. We turned to the door in surprise, but nothing could've prepared us for what we saw there.

Cousin Gabrielle had returned.

12

On instinct, my hands flew to my neck to cover the Elizabeth necklace, as if to protect it from my thieving cousin. But it was too late; she had already seen it. Her red lips fell into a pout as she waggled her finger at Mum. "I *told* you to wait for me!" she scolded.

"Gabrielle! What are you doing here?" Mum asked coldly. Her voice was strong as steel as she put her arm around my shoulders, all traces of tears wiped away and forgotten.

Gabrielle looked puzzled. "I am here for the birthday, of course," she said as she flounced across the room, squishing herself onto the window seat between Mum and me. "Here, little Betsy. I have brought you a present."

With a flourish, Gabrielle reached into her valise and, to my astonishment, withdrew a jewel box that was nearly the twin of the one I'd just received . . . except it was red, not blue. I eyed Gabrielle with suspicion. It was almost too good to be true. And yet . . . I wouldn't know for certain until I—

"Open it. Open it!" Gabrielle said impatiently.

My hands were trembling as I took the box from her. I fumbled with the tarnished clasp but finally, finally, slipped the hook out of the loop and gingerly lifted the lid. It was nestled within the shiny satin folds, and I recognized it at once, though I'd never seen it before.

Rubies glittering like embers, gold gleaming like a burnished sunset, a delicate chain, a half-heart pendant. Yes, it was the Katherine necklace, right here at Chatswood Manor, right here in my hands.

Mum and I gasped at the same time, which made Gabrielle clap her hands as she hooted in delight. My eyes darted back and forth, looking from the Katherine necklace to Cousin Gabrielle and back to the Katherine necklace again.

"I—I—how did—" I stammered.

But Mum was much more direct. "What is the meaning of this?" she demanded.

Gabrielle's laughter died. "I have brought the girl the Katherine necklace," she said. "It is her birthday gift."

"Gabrielle, you're going to have to do better than that if you expect to receive a welcome under this roof," Mum said. "How did it come to be in your possession?"

"I bought it from that handsome American, Patrick O'Brien," Gabrielle said nonchalantly. "Why are you so angry, Beth?"

"*I* was supposed to buy it from him!" Mum said, her temper flaring. "We had an arrangement and you—you *tricked* him and you went *behind my back*—"

Gabrielle waved her hand in the air. "Beth, Beth, you are making a fuss over nothing," she said. "Yes, I suppose I tricked Mr. O'Brien into selling me the necklace. But only because I so very desperately desired to give it to Betsy for her birthday."

"But why?" I asked. "Why the *Katherine* necklace, of all things? Surely you know it could never belong to me—"

Gabrielle grabbed my hand. "No, Betsy, you are the *only* one who should have it," she said firmly. "I will explain everything."

"Good," Mum said. "Because my patience is wearing thin."

Gabrielle looked pained, but for once she didn't have a clever retort on the tip of her tongue. Instead, she said, "The main reason that I wanted to be here for Betsy's birthday was to make amends. It is . . . it is the shame of my life, you know, Beth. The way I almost ruined your twelfth birthday. *Ugh,* what a dreadful little brat I was. Spoiled rotten!"

I saw Mum's face soften. "It was a long time ago," she said. "Water under the bridge, Gabrielle."

"Still, I wanted to make it right," Gabrielle said. "So I thought and I thought until—*eureka!* But wait. I am getting ahead of myself."

She closed her eyes and pressed her hand to her heart. "Beth, I know you remember our dear great-grandmother Cecily. When she died, I was beside myself. I could not eat for *days* and *days.* Not a single bite!"

"Yes," Mum said, nodding. "It was very sad."

"So our country house sat vacant for ten years after Cecily passed away," Gabrielle continued. "And at last, I decided to sell it. I *love* living in Paris, you know. The country life is not for me. But first I had to figure out what to do with everyone's effects. *Maman's* old dresses, Papa's old papers, all the books in the library, even some things that had belonged to Cecily—for example, her old letters. I read them all, including one from Elizabeth Chatswood, dated 1848. And when you read the letter, you will understand *why* it was so very important for Betsy to receive the *Katherine* necklace. Here. I have it with me. It's right—"

"Stop," Mum interrupted her.

Gabrielle and I both stared at Mum.

"This is a family secret that *I* need to tell Betsy," continued Mum. "Please, Gabrielle, you must respect that."

Gabrielle's mouth dropped open in shock. "You *knew*?" she cried. "You *knew* and you never told me?"

"Told you what?" I asked. Then I turned to Mum. "What is she talking about?"

Mum looked torn—but she didn't say anything.

"Please, Mum!" I begged. "You've got to tell me!"

"She has a right to know, Beth," Gabrielle said.

At last Mum reached for my hands and held them both in hers. "This is an old family secret, Beth," Mum said in a soft voice. "Almost as old as the Elizabeth and Katherine necklaces themselves."

My heart was racing. *Is this it?* I wondered. *The big birthday secret that Mum promised to tell me?* I tried to take a deep breath to steady my nerves, but it didn't help.

"You know, of course, that Elizabeth and Katherine received these necklaces for their twelfth birthday in 1848," Mum replied. Then she reached over to the jewel box in my lap. "May I?"

"Yes, yes," I said, fidgeting with the pendant of the Elizabeth necklace; I'd been wearing it for only a few moments, and already it felt like a part of me. "Go on."

Mum carefully removed the Katherine necklace from its case. She held it high so that its rubies glittered in the morning sun. "The truth is somewhat different from the story you've always been told," she continued. "The truth is that Elizabeth Chatswood received the *ruby* necklace . . . not Katherine."

I wasn't sure that I'd heard correctly. My hand clutched the sapphire-studded pendant around my neck. "The ruby necklace?" I repeated.

"Yes, darling. And Katherine received the sapphire

necklace . . . the one you're wearing now."

"But . . . that doesn't make sense," I said in confusion. "Are you saying that the twins switched necklaces? Why would they do that?"

"I have the same question," Gabrielle spoke up. "In her letter to Cecily, Elizabeth wrote in great detail about her love for her ruby necklace. Why would she trade with Katherine?"

"So you don't know the full secret, then," Mum said, looking surprised . . . and perhaps relieved.

"Go on, Mum. Tell us," I said. "I'm dying to know!"

"Yes, Beth. Out with it!" added Gabrielle.

Mum bit her lip before she shook her head. "Betsy, I'm going to ask you to wait a bit longer," she said. "This is a family secret that you and Kay should hear together—the way that Aunt Kate and I always dreamed."

I was barely able to hide my disappointment. *A bit longer?* I thought. *That doesn't make any sense. Since Uncle Joseph and Aunt Kate canceled their trip to England, who knows when Kay and I will finally be together . . . unless . . . what Mum's trying to say is . . .*

When I looked up at Mum, her eyes were twinkling

with merriment. "Yes, Betsy," she said as though she could read my mind. "We're going to America for Kay's birthday!"

"Oh, Mum!" I shrieked as I threw my arms around her neck. "Thank you!"

"You're welcome, darling," Mum replied, squeezing me tight. "And I've been thinking that the money we put aside for your ball could be just as well spent on throwing a ball for you *and* Kay—to celebrate your twelfth birthdays together."

"A ball in America?" I cried. "For both of us?"

"If you'd like that."

"Oh, would I!"

Then a new thought crossed my mind. "I have a question," I said. "If Cousin Gabrielle wasn't stealing the telegrams and bills . . . then who was?"

Gabrielle looked surprised. "*Me?* You thought *I* was stealing your mother's private correspondence?"

I squirmed uncomfortably. "Well . . . for information about the Katherine necklace," I tried to explain. "And . . . there was a rumor that you . . . had designs on Chatswood Manor."

"Why on *earth* would I want the Chatswood

inheritance?" Gabrielle asked incredulously. "After I sold our country estate, I have enough money to last me through *two* lifetimes!"

Then she burst out laughing. "But I suppose I can't blame you for your suspicion," she continued. "I probably deserved it!"

"I have one more secret to share with you today, Betsy," Mum said. "It turns out that Juliette was the culprit."

I gasped. "Juliette?"

"I'm afraid so. A few weeks ago, Maggie caught her prowling about the hallway near my bedroom," Mum explained. "Of course, there was absolutely no reason for Juliette to be there, so Maggie rightfully brought the matter to my attention and has kept me apprised of Juliette's behavior ever since."

"Is that why Maggie's been to see you so much?" I asked. "I thought she was trying to get me in trouble!"

"In trouble for what?" Mum asked, raising an eyebrow.

I grinned sheepishly. "Well . . . never mind. I guess I owe Maggie an apology. But, Mum, how did you find out that Juliette was stealing the telegrams?"

"Last night, to my reluctance, I ordered Mr. Embry to conduct a search of the servants' quarters," Mum said. "That's why I couldn't stay with you at bedtime. And lo and behold, an entire cache of stolen papers was found beneath Juliette's mattress . . . including the letter that you'd been writing to Kay."

"*Juliette* stole my letter?" I cried. "But why?"

Mum shrugged. "Who can say? She obviously had an unhealthy preoccupation with the workings of Chatswood Manor. I'd kept a very close eye on Juliette at the start of her employment, you know, especially after what happened with her sister." Mum paused as she looked over at Gabrielle. "I'm sure you remember your former lady's maid, Helena."

"Do you mean to tell me that your *chef* is Helena's sister?" Gabrielle exclaimed. "It's a wonder she didn't try to poison me!"

"Wait," I said to Mum. "*You* knew about Juliette's sister?" Then I turned to Gabrielle. "Helena was *your* lady's maid? How come you didn't see a resemblance when you scolded Juliette?"

Gabrielle looked baffled. "Scolded Juliette? What are you talking about? I never saw her in my life."

Suddenly, I realized that Juliette's story about Gabrielle's mistreatment was just one of many untrue things she'd said.

"Yes, Betsy. Juliette's sister is the same lady's maid who almost cost Shannon her position," Mum told me. "Of course, I had a thorough investigation conducted on Juliette's background before I hired her. But I didn't think it was fair to deny her employment for a crime her sister had committed. And over the months, she appeared to be a dependable, trustworthy employee. Now, of course, I think that she was merely biding her time. It wouldn't surprise me in the least to learn that Juliette was responsible for all those rumors about Chatswood Manor's supposed financial troubles. I'm sure that's why she stole your letter, Betsy. She was probably worried that you were about to discover her secret scheme."

"I thought Juliette was my friend," I said, feeling foolish. "What will happen to her now?"

"She is already gone," Mum replied. "After the papers were discovered in her room, Juliette confessed everything. I dismissed her on the spot. I wasn't about to have anyone at Chatswood Manor who might ruin your birthday, Betsy. Though I *am* sorry that your birthday dinner will feature only plain fare."

I started to laugh. "That's all right," I told Mum. "I'd already requested roast chicken and buttered peas!"

"What? No blini?" For a moment, Gabrielle looked disappointed. "Well, if that's what suits you. Now, tell me, Betsy—which necklace will you keep? The sapphires or the rubies? An agonizing decision, to be sure!"

I reached behind my neck to unfasten the clasp of the sapphire necklace. Then I placed it beside the ruby one. They were so lovely together, just the way they must've looked when Elizabeth and Katherine had received them nearly a hundred years ago.

But Gabrielle was wrong. It wasn't a difficult decision to make at all.

"This is the necklace that my mother wore," I told Gabrielle as I held up the sapphire pendant. "And my grandmother, my great-grandmother, and my great-great-grandmother. I can't imagine wearing anything else."

And I had the feeling that Cousin Kay would agree when we returned the ruby necklace to her for her twelfth birthday . . . in just a few short weeks!

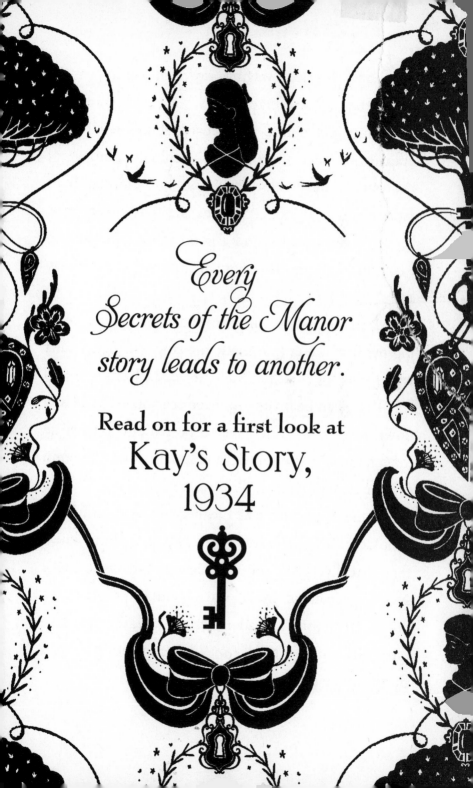

Every Secrets of the Manor story leads to another.

Read on for a first look at

Kay's Story, 1934

"Betsy!" I cried, waving my arm wildly in the air. "Betsy! Down here!" Ever since the enormous steamship had pulled into Boston Harbor, I'd been craning my neck in hopes of catching a glimpse of my cousin, Betsy Northrop, and her mother, Beth Etheridge-Northrop. At last, the passengers had begun to disembark—and a good thing, too, because I couldn't wait another moment to finally meet Betsy and Aunt Beth!

Mom slipped her arm around my shoulder, pulling me into a hug that made me stop waving. "I can't wait to see them either, Kay," she said. "But there's no way Betsy can hear you—or even see you—all the way down here. We'll just have to be patient for a little longer. I'm sure she and Beth will walk down the ramp as soon as they can."

I smiled sheepishly as I leaned my head on Mom's shoulder. I knew she was right, of course, and I knew that it really wasn't proper behavior for me to make such a spectacle of myself, waving and shouting on the docks. But patience had never come easily to me—especially not now of all times, when meeting Cousin Betsy was just moments away!